FINDING A VOICE

KIM HOOD grew up in British Columbia, Canada. After earning degrees in psychology, history and education, she wandered through a few countries before making the west coast of Ireland home.

Her eclectic work experience in education, therapy and community services has presented endless opportunity to observe a world of interesting characters. She has always had a passion for trying to understand life from the perspective of those on the fringes of society.

Finding A Voice is Kim's first novel.

FINDING A VOICE

KIM HOOD

THE O'BRIEN PRESS
DUBLIN

First published 2014 by
The O'Brien Press Ltd,
12 Terenure Road East,
Rathgar,Dublin 6,
Ireland.
Tel: +353 1 4923333;
Fax: +353 1 4922777
E-mail: books@obrien.ie.
Website: www.obrien.ie

ISBN: 978-1-84717-543-4

8 7 6 5 4 3 2 1

18 17 16 15 14

Cover image courtesy of iStockphoto
Printed and bound by CPI Group (UK) Ltd, Croydon, CR0 4YY
The paper in this book is produced using pulp from managed forests

The O'Brien Press receives assistance from

DEDICATION

For Amanda, Jonathan and Shirley who remind me every day that life is a privilege not to be wasted.

ACKNOWLEDGEMENTS

Most sincere thanks to: my fab first readers (Fran, Emma, 'Eve's Mum' Siobhan, 'market' Siobhan, and 'our' Siobhan); my agent Svetlana (how lucky am I!); my editor Helen (for 'getting' the story so right); to my family in Canada (for believing in me and waiting patiently for the book); and most of all to Karl and Jaia (for unwavering support and love through the ups and especially the downs of living with a writer).

CHAPTER ONE

One, two, three, four. I started counting the steps as soon as my feet left the drive. At first, walking so quickly I could barely keep count, but counting nonetheless. Pouring all of my consciousness into keeping count, blocking any other thought out. Thirteen, fourteen, fifteen. Opening one finger at a time when I got into the two-syllable numbers to make sure I didn't lose track of how many steps I had taken.

Keeping count was a kind of habit for me now; each step took me further from my house, where I couldn't control the chaos, to my place of safety. On the days when I couldn't cope anymore, I could literally count on this measured trek to bring me to the place where I could let go – if only for a short while.

One hundred and sixty-five, one hundred and sixty-six. I knew that by the time I reached two hundred the path veering off the right shoulder of the lane would be in sight and the feeling of suffocation would start to give way to great gulping breaths as I started to breathe properly again, feeling the dizzying rush of air that followed depriving my body of oxygen. When I reached the path I knew I would be okay, and I slowed down, relieved that I was far enough from home to begin to let in feelings.

Two hundred and ninety, two hundred and ninety-one. Sometimes, when I entered the cool quiet of the trees it was enough to know that I was going to my safe place and I'd feel only relief, or maybe a little sadness. A few silent tears would be all that I needed to let go – here where I didn't need to be strong for anyone. I would feel the great spruce trees taking my sadness to their tips and as I walked I could stop counting, and let the trees slowly fill me up with the strength of their lifetimes of surety. On these days the walking was enough.

But today was not one of those days. Today was one of the especially bad ones. Today was one of the days that smashed every good day that had come before it and, just for good measure, stomped on all hope for any good days to come. Today I needed to keep counting; I didn't feel it was safe to let in any feelings yet.

Just for a couple of hours, I had let myself forget to worry. It had started with science class. We had started biology, and today was the first day of dissections. I shared a desk with a girl who had smiled warmly at me for the last six weeks that we had perched side by side on our lab stools. Sarah, her name was. And until today I had known little more about her. I knew she had to have come from either Cedarside Elementary or Blue River, or maybe even was new to the town.

In fact, I suspected that she must be entirely new, because she didn't seem to know anyone else in the science class, and yet she seemed really nice, and, well, normal, even popular material. She had a pencil case that I quite envied, and a whole host of gel pens that she took tidy notes with in some sort of system of colour coding.

Even though she smiled at me each time we arrived to science class, we hadn't spoken more than a few words to each other before. Until now the class had consisted of review, which meant a whole lot of looking up at the white board, while the teacher wrote up facts and displayed diagrams, scattering questions in between that a few students keen to impress early in the year dutifully answered with raised hands. Both Sarah and I had kept to the background, only answering questions if we had to, even though we usually got them right.

These review lessons had typically been followed by eyes-to-the-paper worksheets, again not offering much opportunity to chat at all. Not that I was used to idle chat with my classmates. I didn't expect anyone to want to talk to me anymore.

On the first day of middle school I'd walked into my first class early and sat in the middle row, ready to talk to the first kid who sat by me. Surely there would be new kids, ones who wouldn't know that most people had avoided me in elementary school. But it seemed everyone who came in after me came in a group. They sat together, talking about the fun things they'd done in the summer. Not one person had looked at me. After that I arrived to classes just before the last bell.

So I was sort of pleased with how comfortable Sarah seemed to be with me. It was okay that we didn't talk much.

But today had been the beginning of the dissection unit. Everyone in the science class seemed to be anticipating ghoulish autopsy, and so there was almost a carnival atmosphere in the grade 8, block H science class. Notebooks were away while pairs of stool-perchers jostled each other to collect the unfamiliar tools of dissection: tray filled with scarred black wax, silver scalpel, six chunky pins, a dentist-type probe. And then the teacher came around with a jar of medicinal-smelling eyeballs, plunking one into each wax tray, imploring everyone at the same time to *'please people, do not touch your eye until I have passed them all out and given further instructions.'*

Even I caught the spirit of the class when one of the boys' unheeding pokes to his eyeball sent it soaring into the right ear of the girl sitting ahead of him. The excitement in the class erupted, with everyone roaring with laughter. I had to hold my ribs to stop the stitch that developed from laughing so much.

Sarah's polite friendliness cracked open, revealing her talkative, witty interior. And I just got caught up in it.

'Where do you think they get these eyeballs from? Do

you think there's a farm of blind sheep somewhere, all in the name of teaching us dissection?' Sarah questioned me.

'For sure!' I responded. 'But that's not all. They use the sheep to teach the guide dogs too.'

For the first time in a long time I felt like a normal kid, one who might look forward to what she was doing on the weekend rather than worrying about what she might have to face when she got home.

This was exactly what I had hoped for in starting middle school.

Mom had even taken me shopping for new clothes the week before school started. I'd been a bit worried about spending the money, so I'd suggested going to the bargain shop, thinking I could at least find some generic t-shirts and jeans that would pass as cool enough.

'For middle school! They'll crucify you if you show up in the wrong gear!" she'd surprised me by saying. 'No, we have to go to the mall.'

What could I say? Sometimes Mom's impulsiveness was a good thing.

'Look, Jo! Perfect for the first disco!' she'd say, holding up something a granny would wear, just to make me laugh. Then she'd ask me to pick something and I would try to sneak a look at the price tags before taking something from the hanger. In the end she went down the racks tearing off the price tags so that I had to pick stuff I liked, no matter how much it cost. And even when she rolled her eyes at my choices, she let me buy what I wanted.

I looked down at the cool top and jeans I had on now. I liked them, but clothes hadn't been an instant fix. It had been nearly three weeks since school started and not much had changed from elementary. I was still mostly ignored, and occasionally whispered about.

Sarah nudged me with the end of her metallic silver pen.

'What do you think of James there?' she pointed to a boy two rows ahead of us. 'I think he is adorable in a sort of puppy-dog cute way. He's a bit short now, but give him half a year – he'll be gorgeous.'

'I suppose,' I said, surveying the room and picking out another boy before whispering to her, 'Don't you think he looks more interesting in a I-am-profound-and-mysterious sort of way?'

Sarah wrinkled her nose, and I was almost afraid I had ruined it by saying something weird until she grinned.

'There won't be any problem with us liking the same boys, Jo!'

Usually when someone was this nice to me I would be wondering if she was talking to me just to see if I mentioned something about what it was like to have a crazy mother. Or I would start to get worried that someone might mention a hangout in town or a band that I didn't know about, because outside of school, I never talked to anyone and sure never went anywhere. But with Sarah I didn't think to worry, for some reason.

By the time the bell rang, I was pretty sure we were starting to be friends. She might even wave to me if we passed each other in the halls.

And then, wonder of wonders, Sarah stopped me before I left with, 'Hey, why don't you come over to my house this afternoon?'

I didn't want to let go of this feeling of fitting in. I was afraid it might be gone tomorrow, so I said yes. This was middle school now. This was my new start. Before the school year began hadn't I fervently sent wishes and prayers on the wings of a few religions along this very theme? *'Please let my new haircut and definitely-in-style jeans make people forget they thought I was weird last year!' 'Please let me meet new kids who know nothing about me!'* And mostly, *'Please help me learn to be normal!'*

So I had gladly followed Sarah to her mother's silver four-door sedan when the final bell rang. It had seemed the most natural thing in the world to sink into the grey leather rear seat and click the seat belt into place; assuring Sarah's mother that I would of course ring my mom this instant to ask whether it was okay to go to Sarah's until five. And it had even felt almost normal to be ringing Mom on the cell phone that I hardly ever used, to ask just that. The twinge of relief when her phone went to voicemail should have given me the first reminder that there was a reason I never went to other people's houses. But it didn't.

And even two hours later, when I was walking up the steps to my house after being dropped off by Sarah's mom, I felt like skipping I was so happy. It had been a glorious afternoon of sampling Sarah's music, flipping through magazines and munching Doritos. The only conflict was when Sarah threw a shoe at her younger brother to chase him out of her room. All was lightness and smiles. Today it had seemed so easy to replace six years of craziness with one afternoon of normalness.

Until I walked in the door of course.

Five hundred and four, five hundred and five, five hundred and six. If I stopped counting I wouldn't make it. Fear and rage and the hint of something more sinister – losing control – coursed through me. And so I walked more quickly, shoving my closed fists into my coat pockets and shoving any feelings away with my metronome of counting.

Shove as I might, the reality of today was too raw to ignore. As soon as I opened the front door I knew that I had made a mistake in not coming straight home as I usually did. Mom was sitting at the kitchen table in the chair directly facing the side door that I always used to come in. We both used it; not only because our shoes and coats lined the wall beside the door, but because we somehow had lost the only front door key ages ago and hadn't bothered to change the lock.

So it was obvious that Mom had chosen that seat to have the most impact. And it worked.

Dominating her face was a wide smile, almost frozen in its rigidity. If her face was a snapshot framed and on the wall the smile might have been judged as warm or happy. In real life, her continuing to smile without altering one muscle in her face through the several seconds it took me to hang up my coat set warning bells ringing. She was sitting, legs crossed properly, dressed in an A-line skirt with red pumps and a matching red blouse. Her hair was neatly secured back. And she was flipping very casually through a recipe book.

'Hello, sweetie pie.' Not a pet name my mother ever used. She didn't tend to use pet names at all, but when she did they were always some esoteric comparison to a wild animal that she threw out without explanation, usually not more than once. The last one, some weeks ago, had been 'dog shark' when I got up from the sofa to head to bed – as in, 'Go on, my little dog shark. See you tomorrow.' While I wasn't usually sure what Mom's names made reference to, they were never sentimental – and never mainstream. So 'sweetie pie' was the second clue that this afternoon was not going to be an easy one.

'Hi, Mom.'

One mode of survival was to simply pretend everything was normal. In fact, it would look pretty normal to someone who didn't know my mom.

15

'Where's your new friend, Jo? I thought you might bring her for dinner?' The smile had not wavered. Her tone was unnervingly light. 'I'm just looking through this recipe book now. I'm sorry that dinner isn't in the oven yet, but usually I don't cook. Accidents can happen to me!' Laughing slightly, Mom held up both her wrists that were crisscrossed with raised, curved scars.

I took a deep breath and came to sit beside her, taking one of her hands as I did so. I could do this; I could bring this afternoon back to manageable. Over the years I had learned the tricks that could calm Mom's anxieties and make the world just right enough for her to cope. I only had to stay calm and pick the right trick.

'Can I make us some pancakes? And those good sausages that are in the freezer.'

If she would take this lifeline, this assurance that all was still well in our small world, then I was sure that we could manoeuvre through the evening.

'But I've found this recipe for Asian chicken. Here, see, page 173, look, see? A proper mother cooks dinners like Asian chicken.' She was up and in the kitchen, opening cupboards, taking out pans, assembling various ingredients, as if she did this on a regular basis. And my heart sank; literally it felt as if my heart was falling into my stomach. Because this was new, and I didn't know how to counter it, to bring Mom back to apathetic depression where we both knew how to interact and get through each day. This meant that I had crossed some imaginary line of 'what sent Mom over the edge'. All that I could do now was to play along with it, irrationally hoping that she truly was trying to be a 'normal' mother, but knowing at my core that this was going nowhere good.

'I have some English homework,' I tried desperately. 'It's an essay on *The Lord of the Flies*. After dinner can you help me pick which topic to write on?' There was no response to this and now Mom was humming some indecipherable song. So I did indeed take some homework out of my backpack and begin to half-heartedly finish off the math assignment I had started in class earlier in the day. I tried to ignore the fact that frozen chicken, straight from the freezer, had been covered in oil and been left to somehow cook in the fry pan while Mom went about attacking a pepper on the chopping block. Despite the unorthodoxy of her cooking methods, it did seem that she had a plan, and so maybe this might be a good thing. I couldn't remember the last time Mom had cooked anything more complicated than beans on toast. *Maybe this was both of our new starts,* I tried to tell myself, fervently willing myself to believe it. I put my head down and settled into completing my math in all seriousness.

The song Mom hummed became progressively louder, until I knew the song and she began to sing short refrains of *Sweet Child o' Mine* at the top of her voice. There was more chopping and more cupboards opening, but unfortunately no chicken-turning. The chicken, frozen as it was, began to burn, but I didn't know whether to intervene or let her continue to play her adopted part of domestic parent. I felt the familiar tension creep up my spine, the tension that sent my body into flight mode when I no longer could predict what would happen next.

That was the worst. The depression was comfortable at this point. The crying and imagined illnesses were exhausting, but familiar. The curses and hurled put-downs hurt my soul, but I was tough enough to heal. Even the euphoric happiness that inevitably led to a sudden plummet into darkness was bearable. But this, this knife-edge of control that Mom occasionally found – whether it was in silence, or feigned camaraderie – could only be devastating.

The chicken began to burn in earnest, and still she focused on chopping and humming.

'Mom?' I tried hesitantly. 'I think the chicken is ready.'

Wham!!! The frying pan, chicken first, flew across the room with such velocity it seemed someone twice Mom's size had thrown it. I jumped up, even before the pan hit the wall opposite me, and instinctively edged to the door.

'Where were you!!' she hurled the words as an accusation, definitely not a question. 'I can't handle the worry! You *know* I can't handle the worry!'

And I was out the side door. Out the door, counting the steps. Mom could survive this fleeing. She would know that

I would be back, calm enough for both of us. But though I couldn't process much in my flight mode, I did understand that she couldn't survive a normal adolescent after-school visit to a friend's house. What had I been thinking? Who knows what she was up to now, and it was all my fault.

Eight hundred and ten, eight hundred and eleven. I reached the river, high with the recent rains. And now I stopped counting, skirting the river bank, making my way up the kilometre or so until I reached the sandbank that was my front garden when the weather was good. Behind this was a little glen, enclosed with dense cedar trees, but open in the middle. A little oasis that nobody else seemed to know about. But the best part of all was the little log cabin on the far side of the opening. It was barely big enough to even count as more than a shed, and it was mostly falling down. But it was my haven. And there, entering the door and not even making it to one of the ancient chairs, I collapsed, letting out great heaving sobs in the only place in the world where I could.

CHAPTER TWO

When I woke the following morning it was underneath a blanket of dread. It hadn't been an easy night. Eventually the guilt of leaving Mom in distress had cut through my own pit of misery and I had returned home in the near dark.

I found Mom pacing the house, half-prepared dinner still strewn across the kitchen, mumbling to herself.

'I'm not fit to be a mother. Look at the state of me. Can't even cook a dinner. She was right. She was right. She was right.'

She had discarded the red pumps and was marching in bare feet, despite the sharp remains of a glass that seemed to have followed the pan after I made my exit. Likewise, her hair was free from its clip and was beginning to look a bit wild from her frantic hands running through it.

I was prepared. I'd left my own emotions in my hideaway, and now I could throw myself into making things all right for Mom. I just had to find a way to calm her down, and I could do it. I'd been doing it my whole life.

'She is always right. *Can't be a mother,* she said. *You'll ruin her. She'll end up like you,* she said.' Mom was still ranting. At least this was a theme that I recognised well.

'It's okay, Mom! I'm not ruined. Grandma is wrong. See, I'm okay!'

I walked calmly to her and took both her hands in my own. I tried to hold her gaze, but her eyes were still frantic, scanning the room wildly and she dropped my hands to pick up the dishcloth she'd spotted. She then sprang across the room to scrub the streaks of dripping brown sauce that crisscrossed the refrigerator. It was as if I was not even in the room.

'Please, come sit down, Mom. Remember how I need help with homework?'

I gathered up my books from the table and looked through them, finding the page I had been handed in English class earlier that day. If anything could pull Mom from the dark topic of *How Grandma had felt it would be best for Mom to give Jo up for adoption* it would be thinking about *Which tribe in* The Lord of the Flies *would you have chosen to join? Why? What do you think the two tribes represent?* Literature was her life. I only wished that my class was reading something a bit lighter; a little comedy would have been better than the darkness of *The Lord of the Flies*.

But nothing had worked. Not the promise of discussing my assigned book as allegory, not the pancakes and sausages that I made to replace the ruined dinner, not cleaning up the mess that Mom had left, not imploring her to join me on the sofa for the sitcoms we liked to watch together to wind down our weekdays.

Instead, Mom continued to walk the house, if you could call it walking. It was more like she was terribly late for an appointment in the next room, and then when she would arrive there she would remember that she had left the iron on back in the last room she had been in. The mumbling eventually stopped, but running her hands through her hair did not. Her only acknowledgement that I was there was the occasional pleading look and, 'I'm sorry. I'm sorry I'm your mother.'

By ten o'clock I was starting to get very worried. Even on a good day Mom could have times when she acted as oddly, but only for short periods and I would know how to get her back to the routines of the day – eating the dinner I usually cooked and watching some television, both of us complaining about how bad the shows were.

This was too long. This was all too familiar.

By eleven o'clock I was rooting through Mom's bedside table, looking through the boxes and bottles that were the lifeline that kept her on this side of reality. I knew what I was looking for; I was looking for a small, clear, zip-lock packet.

This was against 'The Rules'. The cupboard was supposed to be locked, and the key kept hidden from me. It was part of Mom's home-care plan, the one that allowed me to stay with her, despite the risks identified by our social worker. Teens and medications for hallucinations and wild mood swings are apparently seen to be a dangerous combination. The drug I was looking for was especially to be kept out of reach.

I was breaking another rule as well – the rule that I was to call the mental health crisis team nurse when Mom wasn't well. And Grandma. I wasn't to be in the house when Mom spiralled away from the sane world.

The thought of making that call made my stomach churn – I couldn't do it.

For a moment I hesitated, hearing the words the social worker had said to me the last time we had met. *You know your mom will be unwell again, don't you, Jo? You can't stop it. We'll just be ready for it.*

But she had been so well for almost a year. This *was* all my fault, wasn't it? I had stepped outside the pattern that kept Mom on track when I accepted an invitation to Sarah's house.

And besides, it wasn't exactly easy to tell when Mom was actually going over the edge – as opposed to her normal weirdness. It was just a bad night.

So instead I searched through the myriad of drugs until I found what I was looking for – Ativan, the tiny miracle pill that promised sleep for us both. And just as I had hoped, when I handed it to Mom in the little plastic medication cup, she had taken it placidly and placed it under her tongue, grasping the promise of her fears and anxieties melting away until the morning at least.

But things were not better in the morning. I knew it the minute I opened my eyes and heard the vacuum start up in the living room. It was a definite bad sign. When Mom was as well as she could be, she never stirred from her bed until noon.

Ever since I could remember I had got myself ready in the morning and laid out Mom's meds before I left for school. I didn't exactly know what they were supposed to do. Sometimes I didn't even know the names of the meds if they were new to the mix. What I did know was that when she didn't take that multicoloured handful of pills every day it was a sure way for our lives to quickly spiral out of control.

And even when she did take them as they were supposed to be taken they never seemed to be a miracle cure for long. I feared the vacuuming at 7a.m. was a bad sign – a sign that the mix of medications would have to change. I didn't remember a time when bad things didn't happen before the change of pills happened.

It was a long, long day.

In history I had to madly finish the math homework I hadn't completed the night before.

At lunch time Sarah walked toward me with an expectant smile and a wave, and I could only manage a half smile and a shrug. I thought about veering down a side hallway to avoid her, but she was right in front of me before I could.

'Hey, Jo,' she greeted. She stood waiting for me to say something back.

'I've gotta go.' I tried to think of some place I needed to be, some excuse to get me away from this. Finally I just pointed down the hall to my left. 'This way.'

Then I just ran in the direction I had pointed.

I felt sick and guilty and worried all at once – a wave that started in my stomach and rose to set my heart beating fast.

I didn't know why I hadn't been able to just say 'hello'. Yesterday it had been all that I hoped for – the promise of a normal friendship, of being liked. Today – that hope seemed to be the very cause of Mom's problem, like if I talked to Sarah I was somehow going to make her worse. Again, I heard the social worker's words *You can't stop it*. I wanted to believe her. I wanted to go back and find Sarah, but some-how I just couldn't.

In the end I took my sandwich and my English binder out to the very back of the school where I knew I would meet no one and I could avoid analysing my feelings. I tried to scratch out a decent essay for English class. The couple of bites I attempted to take of my sandwich were so ill-received by my stomach that I gave up on eating.

The afternoon wasn't much better. I was asked to read a passage aloud in English and couldn't seem to get past a sentence at a time without stumbling on words. In PE it was field hockey and I couldn't even keep up with the play, never mind have any hope of actually being a contributing team member. I didn't have to look up from the ground to know that the girls assigned to the side I was on were rolling their eyes.

By the time I walked in the door at home all I wanted to do was turn on the TV and turn off my brain for a couple of hours.

The phone was ringing and Mom was not answering it, so I did. Big mistake.

'Hello?'

My heart started beating faster when Grandma answered, 'Well, I was wondering when you might arrive to pick up. How are you, in any case?'

'Yeah I'm good, Grandma. And you?' I hoped I sounded calm and unconcerned.

Much as I feared Grandma's quick and harsh judgements that she threw like daggers without thought to where they landed, I was always amazed at how accurately she was able to assess how well – or how unwell – Mom was. And today something had obviously happened to make her want to check on her daughter's well-being.

'I'm as well as can be expected,' Grandma snipped. 'Where is your mother? She isn't answering the phone.'

'Um, well I just got in from school. Shall I find her for you?' I really hoped she'd say no. I wasn't at all sure that

Mom was well enough for what we both jokingly called 'The Inquisition'.

'I've three hang-ups from her today. She isn't at her programme, obviously.' She was referring to the drop-in mental health centre where Mom was welcome to come each afternoon.

I wanted to jump to Mom's defence. It wasn't a 'programme'. It was an optional support – as needed. But nothing was optional to Grandma. I doubted she had ever so much as missed brushing her teeth twice a day, because it was what you were supposed to do.

'Grandma, did you know I'm still second from the top in English?' It was a tactic that sometimes worked when she was honing in on Mom's shortcomings. Divert attention.

'Good, but you're to call the first sign it's needed, Jo.' She was onto it, knew that Mom was not coping so well today, but she knew better than to ask me how Mom was. I always said, 'Good.'

Mom was fast asleep in her bed, blinds drawn, two duvets piled on top of her, curled into a ball when I found her. I was relieved – somewhat. At least I could relax in front of the television for a while.

I left her to sleep, quietly crossing the hall into the living room to watch television. The curtains were pulled in here as well, making the room seem darker and more closed than usual. It was a small room anyway, but on all sides the furniture was penned in with bookshelves that reached far up each wall. It wasn't exactly a library. The books were mostly tattered paperbacks, many with missing front covers and all of them filled with notes, highlighted passages and sticky notes protruding from their tops.

In the middle of the floor today there were at least a dozen books off the shelves. There was a short pile of four books, several opened and face down on the carpet, and a few more scattered around the room. I knew better than to move any of them. There was always a method to the madness and touching those books was a sure way to send Mom into a frenzy.

Once, I had met an old friend of Mom's, a friend from her university days. I can remember that he had come for dinner and he and Mom had drunk lots of wine.

At one point Mom had left the room to go to the toilet. The friend had turned to me, where I was sitting quietly in the corner chair trying to be invisible so I wasn't sent to bed, to say, 'Your mom is an encyclopaedia of literary facts, but it's not just theory or theme to her – never was. Her *world* is literature. I don't think she exists outside of the stories she reads.'

It was the sort of conversation I had been raised on. I loved that Mom never talked down to me; she had always talked to me like she would any adult. I didn't care that only a few words of these sorts of talks made sense to me most of the time when I was small, even now sometimes. *I don't think she exists outside of the stories she reads* had made sudden and utter sense to me, though, even several years ago.

I was just settling in to watching an episode of a sitcom I had seen several times before, when Mom appeared at the doorway, looking panicked.

'I can't find it!'

'Can't find what, Mom?' I asked, feeling slightly annoyed that my moment of peace was gone.

'The answer. What ties us all together. It should be here – and I can't find it!' She swept her arm around the room, indicating her menagerie of books.

'Mom, you're tired. You'll find it tomorrow.' I had no idea what she was looking for, but I had learned over time, and many mistakes, not to ask, not to go there. 'No, I won't, Jo. That's my problem. There's me. There's you. There's her. I can't make it fit. I can't find anything to make the three fit!'

'What can I do, Mom?'

'That's just it, Jo. I can't give you the answer!' Her words tumbled out, speeding up more and more. She was pacing again and tapping her hands on her thighs as she did. Her hair was still uncombed, her clothes unchanged, mascara still streaking down her cheeks.

My stomach clenched and churned. I had hoped it was a glitch that some solid sleep would have sorted. Sometimes it did.

29

Instead, Mom got more animated and panicked as the minutes of the evening ticked slowly on. Again, nothing seemed to engage her – not dinner, not conversation, not quiet, not even shouting at her, as I finally resorted to when she sent the medication that I offered her in the cup flying with a deliberate sweep of her arm. At this point it was midnight.

'Stop!' I shouted at her. 'Can't you just stop, please?!'

She just paced on into the kitchen. And I burst into tears. I felt so exhausted and scared and I didn't know what else I could do. Except press the panic button – call the crisis team nurse to say Mom wasn't well. And I couldn't do that to her – no matter how angry I might be with her. I wouldn't call unless I had to. And I didn't have to yet.

So I went to bed and sobbed into my pillow instead. And as worried as I was, I still fell into a deep sleep.

I woke up with my light still on, so I couldn't immediately tell what time it was. What woke me was the sound of some sort of siren. It wasn't until I figured out it was still night because it was dark outside my window that I realised the siren was Mom and she seemed to be wailing.

I stumbled through my bedroom door toward the sound. It was coming from the bathroom. I tried to piece it together before I arrived there, fighting my way out of sleep and dreams. The sound was Mom, and she was crying, sort of, but why?

Suddenly I was wide awake. I knew why before I even

nudged the bathroom door open.

Mom was crouched on the floor, back leaning against the bathtub, knees higher than her head and arms splayed to each side, all the better to display the oozing criss-crossed red lines up both of her forearms. And I knew that I no longer had a choice in bringing in the crisis team.

CHAPTER THREE

Mom had not stopped screaming even when the paramedics injected her in the arm with some sort of drug. Then she was out the door and the silence was louder than the screaming had been. I sat in the living room and counted the seconds until Mom's social worker Francie arrived. She had rung me to tell me she was on her way to stay with me until Grandma could pack some things and drive the three hours from her house to ours. I hadn't realised I was holding my breath until she walked in, settling immediately into the couch beside me.

'She's going to be okay, you know. She'll be sleeping soon, and they'll keep her that way for much of the next couple of days.' Francie always talked this way. No small talk, no protecting me from the details of mental illness, and always answering my questions before I even knew they were my questions. 'Her injuries are superficial – but you know that don't you, kiddo? How are your wounds?'

I let out the air in my lungs.

'Superficial I guess. I think it was my fault anyway.' The confession just slipped out. It was the lack of sleep. My guard was down.

'Jo, I know you love your mom, but the reality is, she has a long, long history of mental health difficulties. You can't cure her – and equally, you can't be responsible for making her worse.'

I felt myself stiffen. Why did she always have to bring this up? The thing that Francie didn't know was that I *could* make days better or worse for Mom. And I had screwed up. If I helped her not to feel stressed about anything, then days were better. Going to Sarah's house had tipped the balance too far in the direction of a *bad* day, one Mom couldn't see beyond.

* * *

I awoke to the voices of Francie and Grandma speaking in the kitchen. My eyes still felt heavy and I wasn't ready to face Grandma, so I closed my eyes and tried to erase the last two days from my mind. It didn't work though, so I decided to just get out of bed.

I padded into the kitchen in my moose slippers. If there was any plus to these episodes of Mom's it was the day or so that I was always awarded to fall into utter comfort.

'Well hello, Goose. Nice to see that we won't just be meeting in the dead of night,' Francie said.

Grandma was typically much more reserved.

'Good afternoon, Jo. I expect you have had a difficult few days. Sit down. I'll make you a cup of tea.'

I figured this must be one of Grandma's Irish things – and it was the one thing that cemented our connection – Grandma and me. The cup of tea. We could certainly never talk about the thing that most often brought us together – Mom's illness. But we could put the kettle on several times in an evening – watch it boil, prepare the cups, the tea bags, the sugar, pass the mugs to each other, sit down at the table together and sip a good cup of tea, passing small talk between us for the time it took to drink it. I readily accepted.

While Grandma got busy making it, Francie filled me in on the arranging she had been doing while I slept.

'So, all going well you can visit your mom on Sunday if you're up for that. Are you up for that?'

'You mean at the hospital?' I startled.

I had never been inside the psychiatric ward before. It had just never been an option to visit. I wasn't sure how I felt about it.

Scared? Would there be lots of crazy people wandering around in hospital gowns talking about the end of the world? Would Mom be one of them?

Relieved? I wouldn't have to worry and wonder how she was.

'It's up to you, kiddo,' Francie offered. 'You just usually ask and we've usually felt you were too young.'

'Ok. I'll go,' I decided on the spot.

'And I've an appointment arranged for you to meet the school psychologist on Monday morning.'

'Why?'

'Frankly, I think you need to process a few things and me telling you isn't going to do it,' she offered, shrugging. 'Besides, I think Dr Sharon needs something a bit more challenging than teenage angst.'

I decided to ignore the whole topic. *Frankly,* I had had quite enough of strangers prying into my life over the years. I wasn't the one who needed fixing after all. Why couldn't there be more effort put into helping Mom?

'Well, that's that. I'd better run and let you two have a bit of time together.'

'Well then. I'm sure we'll be seeing you again soon, Francie. As always, your presence is appreciated in these times.'

Francie gave me one last smile as she left.

I looked around the kitchen, seeing things that usually did not even register, but now seemed to have signs pointing at them. The three hooks by the back door each had far too many coats on them and several had slipped off and lay strewn on the floor on top of piles of shoes. The table was half covered with piles of envelopes, papers, flyers and a few books seeming to keep the piles from cascading down. There was the calendar, turned to February, even though it was September, up on the cupboard. I thought of the contents of the fridge and cupboards and wondered how on earth Grandma would manage to cook one of the traditional meals she usually cooked.

'Here, now.' Grandma handed me a cup of tea.

'Thanks, Grandma.' I took a few sips.

'We've some shopping to do,' she stated, answering the question about dinner, and signalling the end of my all too brief respite from the world.

Grandma had a car, so going shopping was actually not so bad compared to shopping with Mom. Mom didn't drive, so normally grocery shopping took half the day by the time we walked all the way to the main street to catch the bus into town twenty minutes away. There weren't many buses on Sundays either, which was the only safe day to go shopping with Mom because there weren't as many shops open that day. Even so, if I didn't set a strict agenda, shopping tended to go wrong. Like the time she decided to buy the giant – and expensive – jar of spirulena health supplement because she decided on the spot it was somehow healthier to drink green sludge for a week than to eat food. Or the day we stopped at the pet shop to buy and liberate six budgies in the window. We had lived on instant noodles all that week.

So it was nice to just get into Grandma's car and not even have to decide which store we were going to. I simply fetched what she asked me to fetch from the aisles and didn't have to give one thought as to whether we were at the weekly limit yet. Then back into the car, arriving home barely an hour later, warm and dry.

Dinner was the same. Grandma told me what to chop, how to do it, what to put on the table and how to place it. She indicated when it was time to get up to clear the plates after we had finished eating our homemade shepherd's pie and tea. I didn't have to make a single decision. Pleasant in a way.

But after a whole eight hours of it the following day, Saturday nonetheless, I was finding it a lot less pleasant. Saturday was usually a day of leisure in our house. It was the day Mom and I ate only snacks – no cooked meals, opening the fridge and cupboards whenever we felt a bit peckish. We would get up late, read, and watch movies, sometimes not even bothering to change out of our pyjamas at all.

Not so with Grandma here. Saturday started with cleaning windows because the sun was shining. While I didn't mind the thought of clean windows I didn't see the urgency in having clean windows *right now*. It was coming into winter after all, and so most of the time our curtains would be closed to keep the heat in. Couldn't it wait until spring?

Then after lunch Grandma had us in the car and off for a walk along the river walkway. Again, it wasn't that I didn't like being out on a nice day; it was just so regimented. Especially with Grandma marching along like a drill sergeant. By the time we arrived back home in the late afternoon I was fed up with seemingly having my every thought dictated. I ached for the comfort and freedom of my little cabin.

'Grandma, I'm going to go for a small walk,' I announced after the obligatory cup of tea.

'But sure, haven't we just been on a lovely walk?'

'Well, yeah, but, I just …' I struggled for an explanation that would satisfy. I wasn't used to having to ask to go, and I suddenly realised I had never actually told even Mom about the little cabin. That was the kind of relationship we had, short on personal details, at least my personal details.

I had found the cabin quite by accident a couple of years ago. Anyone could find their way down to the river. There was a clear path leading straight down to it from the corner of our road, but from there it was only by skirting along the overgrown river bank for fifteen minutes or so that you came to the small clearing.

It must have been abandoned years ago, but despite having few panes of glass left in the windows and a door that only pulled halfway shut, it was surprisingly dry. Over time I had made some crude repairs to the few broken bits of furniture in it so that I had a table and chair of sorts, and a pretty comfortable armchair. I used to like to pretend I lived there, and I'd brought things to make it homier. It was the only place where I felt truly myself, without any need to adjust how I was feeling or how I was being.

And that was what I needed now. Being with Grandma

was hard for me in a totally different way than being with Mom – but with both of them I had to follow what *they* wanted, all of the time. I could feel my eyes begin to well up and I swallowed hard and took a deep breath. I was determined not to cry.

Grandma just took my chin in her hands then and said, 'Go on then, pet. An hour so. It's better than watching the television.'

I could have hugged her, if it were not that hugs just didn't happen between us.

CHAPTER FOUR

Sunday came too fast. I wasn't sure if I was ready to see Mom yet. I was pretty sure she wouldn't be the mom I wanted to see.

Usually she left me as crazy as she could be, and came back weeks later as sane as she could be.

This was uncharted territory being there for the in-between part. And it was all too raw and real still. The image of Mom in the bathroom with a bloody steak knife beside her, mutilated arms splayed out, was sharp and detailed. There hadn't been time yet for the memory to get fuzzy. By the time I usually saw Mom after an episode I had talked to her several times by phone, her voice becoming less slurred and more coherent as the weeks passed and the medications did their jobs.

Yet Francie was right, through all of those other times I had asked, begged at times, to see her. Especially when I was way younger it had been frightening to have her just 'go away'. I had worried about her, wondered if it was jail she was in because she had been bad, feared I would not see her again.

Despite the many, many talks I had had over the years in all sorts of offices about what happened to Mom being an illness, something she needed medicine for to get better, I had never been able to compare these episodes to any illness I knew. Other illnesses you could talk about without being met with silence and stares. Other illnesses had a set timeline and a surety of how to know when you were better. You didn't get social workers with other illnesses. With other illnesses kids got to visit their parent in the hospital.

Well, now that was going to happen.

Grandma drove the car up to the front door of the hospital and told me that she would meet me in the lobby in one hour.

'You aren't coming in, Grandma?' My stomach did another back flip. It had been doing that all morning.

'I don't believe it would be appropriate, Jo. This is your visit.'

I wondered if she was just as scared as I felt. I didn't, after all, remember Grandma ever going to visit Mom in the hospital.

At the front desk I asked for where to go for Sue MacNamara's room.

'Just one moment, please,' the woman at the desk said. 'That is a secure floor and I need to get clearance.' She pressed some buttons on her phone, spoke to someone and then gave me directions to follow the yellow line to the elevator and press the buzzer on the locked door to the right on floor four.

It was the longest elevator ride ever. At the locked door I hesitated a moment before pushing the button. After waiting for what seemed like ten minutes I was about to press the button again when the door opened and a nurse ushered me in.

'Jo, is it? Sorry for the wait; it's hectic today and I wanted to have my plate cleared so I could bring you straight down without delay.'

I took the scene in. It was an ordinary hospital ward, with a nursing station, a small waiting area with stiff, straight chairs and washed out green corridors branching off in three directions. The only hint that this ward may be somewhat different was the man walking through the waiting area in normal street clothes who stopped to stare at me, breaching unwritten social rules of how strangers behave with one another. It made me feel a little creeped out, but it wasn't as bad as the drooling zombies I had imagined.

'Charlie, go ahead now. They're waiting for you in the rec room,' the nurse dictated to him, and then continued down the middle corridor with me in tow. At the end of this we were buzzed through another door, emerging in a sort of lounge area, with a few plastic-covered armchairs, a shelf with some tattered paperbacks and magazines, and a television at almost ceiling level in one corner. Another whole corner was taken up with a second nursing station, this one completely glassed in.

Mom was sitting in one of the plastic, pale green chairs looking toward the television. She hadn't noticed me yet so I waited for the nurse to direct me to what I should do next.

'Go ahead and pull a chair up with your mom. I'll bring you out a glass of something. It'll have to be whatever is going in the fridge.'

I dragged the nearest plastic-coated armchair across the cold, institutional linoleum to beside Mom and sat down on the edge of it.

'Hi, Mom.' I tucked my hands tightly under my legs and waited, afraid of what would happen next. Slowly Mom turned her head toward me.

'Hey there.' Her eyes didn't seem to focus on me and her face was expressionless. I wasn't sure what I should say or do, but then the nurse returned with two plastic glasses of juice.

'Here you are, Sue and Jo,' she said. 'Sue, you might want to just spend some quiet time watching TV with your daughter.' And to me, 'Your mom is pretty tired right now. The medication she is taking is giving her a rest, but it makes her awfully groggy and she might not feel like talking much.'

'Thanks, Patricia,' Mom slurred, taking the nurse's hand and giving it a squeeze.

So we spent the hour watching a murder mystery show on the little television and talking very little. Those couple of sentences, directing what we should do had made the visit all so normal – like we were at home watching TV after school – only with very bad décor.

I didn't exactly forget to notice that there was a little bead of drool in the corner of Mom's mouth, or that there were bandages peeking out of the sleeves of her hoodie. And there was a woman who came in from the courtyard to have a very loud conversation with a nurse at the desk about how the government had been blackmailing her for years. And I did notice that when the nice nurse left the lounge she had to be buzzed out of the locked door. These were all things that I had imagined and worried about – Mom drugged and not herself, crazy people and locked doors. Yet none of it held quite the same importance or scariness that I'd imagined it would.

After the hour the nurse returned, took our glasses and indicated it was time to go.

'Bye, Mom.' I didn't know what else I should say. *Get better? See you soon?*

'Come here,' Mom said and pulled me in for a hug. My eyes stung with the instant tears of relief that flooded them. It had been a long time since we had shared anything as normal as a goodbye hug. I hugged her back fiercely, trying to open all of my senses so that the memory of this contact might never fade.

CHAPTER FIVE

I had hoped that Francie's arrangement with the school psychologist had been forgotten. Francie hadn't mentioned any time that I was supposed to meet the psychologist, and she hadn't rung over the weekend. Maybe it wouldn't happen?

But it did. During second period Monday I was fetched from class by one of the administrative staff and delivered straight to a small, almost empty room.

'Dr Sharon is on her way. She's hit a bit of traffic, but we expect her any minute now,' the secretary said and then left me to sit in one of three chairs.

It seemed like hours before the doctor – *was a psychologist a doctor?* – arrived. I had almost memorised every word on the three posters on the wall by that time.

Finally the door opened and Dr Sharon came in, looking every bit the doctor or professional type. Her hair was held back in a bun and she wore a navy skirt and matching jacket. Despite being apparently very late she walked in calmly and took her time taking her jacket off. Only when she had methodically arranged a notepad and pen on the table did she fully look at me.

'So,' she started. 'Francie thinks it would be a good idea for us to spend some time together. What do you think of that idea?'

This caught me a bit by surprise.

'Um, well, what do I have to do?'

'Nothing – or everything,' she said. 'It depends what you want from our time.'

'I don't know why Francie wants me to come here. I think I'm okay.'

And then it hit me. Was this about separating me from Mom? Was this the beginning of assessments and preparing me for that? I felt the blood drain from my face and I suddenly felt dizzy.

'Did I not do it right? I called the crisis team! She's been well, she's taken care of me. Really, really! I'm okay. I just made a mistake going over to a girl's house without asking and my mom got worried and then the worry turned bad. But I'm okay and she'll be okay!' The words tumbled out, pleading, begging, hoping that a corner hadn't been turned that could not be retraced.

'Jo,' the doctor stopped me and then waited a minute before continuing slowly. 'This isn't about evaluating you, or your mom, or your home situation. I have nothing to do with social services I promise you. This isn't even about your mom. It's about you.'

I didn't know it at the time, but I would come to learn that this was the most talking that Dr Sharon would ever do without asking a single question.

'So, again, what do you want from our time? What can I help you with right now?'

I thought about the question. I didn't know that anyone could help me with anything. My life wasn't a made-for-TV movie. There wasn't a beginning, middle or an end to the reasons why I was scared and lonely much of the time. It was just – life. Until a few days ago I wouldn't have even felt so awful, even with Mom needing the hospital.

I thought about the last three weeks. Classes weren't so bad, but lunch hours had been miserable so far. Eating my sandwich in the hallway by my locker – alone – while everyone else sat in groups. Walking the halls, trying to look like I was on my way to meet someone. Passing kids I'd gone to elementary school with whispering to kids who had come from other schools, and just knowing they were whispering about me.

But maybe I would have gotten used to that.

It was the dangled carrot of friendship that had ruined everything. Someone who might actually like me and possibly even understand me. Maybe. And now it was worse because for once in my life I could imagine a life I had only ever hoped for. Yet I wasn't sure I could have a friend *and* my mom.

What was I going to do about Sarah? After our meeting on Thursday, she probably thought I was weird. Which, if I wanted to focus on Mom, was a good thing. So why didn't it feel that good?

'I hate lunch hour,' I blurted.

Dr Sharon said, 'Well, let me see what I can do about that.'

And she didn't even ask me why.

* * *

I had expected that it would be at least a week or two before I would see Dr Sharon again – if I did. I was pretty used to meeting with this or that professional, who usually got moved to some other job before I could even remember their name.

So I was completely shocked when a second message came to me during last period on the same day.

This time she was behind the table waiting for me.

'So – lunch hour,' she stated simply. I waited, but no more was offered. After an age she went on to say, 'Tell me about that.'

'I ... it's complicated.' It wasn't really, but how could I say *I want to avoid seeing someone who might actually want to talk to me* without sounding ridiculous.

'In which way?'

I thought of answering. Maybe it would help. But I didn't know where to start, and if I did, would I know where to stop? Instead I just shook my head.

'Right. Well, you're in luck if lunch hour is what you want changed. Is it?'

'Yes.' Finally an easy question.

'Someone needs your help. I'll let him speak for himself, but I can arrange for the help he needs to be during lunch hour.' She handed me a leaflet. 'Take this. Think it over. If it appeals to you, apply with me as a reference. If it doesn't, we can talk about it in a week when I see you next.'

I was far too curious to head back to class without reading what the doctor had handed me. The leaflet was handmade with pasted-on photos and bits of typing in between. The front simply said *Hi, I'm Chris*, and there was a picture of someone in a wheelchair. Not your politically-correct picture of the good-looking guy shooting a basket from a super-slick looking wheelchair either. Even though the boy in the picture was dressed in a suit that could only be for a wedding, and even though he was smiling, there was no disguising the fact that he was obviously not your average kid, only just in a wheelchair. Both his arms were out to the side and in the air and one of his hands was bent inward, with his wrist at an impossible angle and witch-like fingers held stiffly out. His mouth was distorted, despite the smile. But the telling thing was his hair. No self-respecting guy slicked his hair back like it was. Even I, as clueless as I was about fashion or anything cool, knew that.

I opened the pamphlet up. *You might not know me, but I go to your school. I like art and listening to music.* Then there was a photo of an abstract painting and a photo of the boy, with earphones on, same lopsided smile.

On the opposite page, *I'd like to meet new friends who could help me do teenage stuff. Maybe you'd like to contribute something to your community. Maybe you would like some experience and a reference for pursuing a career in special education or social care. Whatever your reasons, any time spent with Chris is most welcome!* This page just had a rainbow of different coloured hands clasped as illustration.

Then on the back:

The Special Ed Department is looking for:

Lunch hour assistants and monitors

'Buddies' to assist in integrated classes (must maintain a B average in assisted class)

In exchange, you get:

Valuable life experience

Getting to know new kids

An opportunity to share your interests/skills

If this interests you talk to Mr Jenkins – Special Education Resource Teacher

I wasn't sure. I didn't have any experience with special ed kids and I had enough of my own weirdness baggage to carry around, without giving everyone another reason to think I was odd. Still, it would give me a place to be every lunch and time to decide what to do about Sarah. What did I have to lose?

CHAPTER SIX

I was nervous walking into the special education wing. Somewhere here I was meeting Mr Jenkins. Was it the rec room? Or the break room? I wasn't sure where exactly.

No one ever came into this wing – the kids here only ever came *out*. The kids from special education were kind of an entity that everyone tried to pretend they didn't see. They were in the occasional class, sitting with their adult assistant in the corner. And whole groups of them came to assemblies, all right. That was when they were most visible. A few of the ignorant kids might mimic some of the special ed kids then, or someone would nervously giggle when a screech was heard in a quiet moment. Mostly though, they were politely ignored. Kind of like me – only they at least had each other and I'd always had to face that on my own.

I didn't even know what Mr Jenkins looked like and how would he know what I looked like? I had only talked to him briefly this morning. I had gone to the office twenty minutes before class had started, clutching my now very creased pamphlet.

'What can I do for you, dear?' the secretary had asked.

'I'd like to speak to Mr Jenkins, but I don't know where I find him.' I had handed the pamphlet to her as if it would explain everything.

'I'll see if he's in his room now.' The secretary had dialled the phone and then handed it to me.

'My name is Jo, and I'm interested in the pamphlet – about Chris.'

'Fantastic!' His response had been almost too enthusiastic. 'We'd hoped you'd join us. How 'bout today? Chris isn't in today, but I could give you a little orientation. If you came the class before lunch, and stayed through lunch, that would give us enough time.'

And that had been it. I had thought there must be some long application or something, checking references, interviews, but no, just – come on down. It had been relatively easy.

I looked into the first two rooms I came to, but didn't see anyone. The rooms were small, with big mats and weird exercise equipment in one and a big mechanical thing with straps hanging down in another. Doubt started to creep in. Was I *sure* this was going to be any easier than just finding a quiet bathroom to hide out in every lunch hour until the end of the year? At least I was familiar with ridicule. In this unfamiliar territory I didn't know what might happen. It occurred to me that these quiet hallways leading to rooms with who knows what in them were more like what I had expected in the hospital wing my mom was in.

I was just about to turn around and walk back out the heavy double doors to normality when a man strode toward me from the other end of the hall.

'Jo!' the man whom I assumed was Mr Jenkins said, sticking out his hand for a handshake. 'Come with me. I'm rushing from one thing to another as usual. Sorry about that, meant to meet you at the door. That's okay though, you found your way and now I'll give you a bit of a tour.'

He talked quickly and seemed to move even faster. I had to speed walk to keep up with him as he led me back down the hall and around a corner.

'So there are twelve students who make this wing their base,' he explained as we walked. 'The goal is to get them all out of here and in classes with the rest of you, but we don't have the resources to make that happen as quickly as we'd like, so most of them are only in a few typical classes.'

I nodded as if I knew what he was talking about. There wasn't time to think about it though because he was still speed walking, stopping briefly to pick up some papers from an office.

'Notices to hand out,' he said. 'I'll kill two birds with one stone while I show you around.' And he was off again.

'Most of our kids have some challenges that you don't see

in regular classes. It could be that they use sign language. It could be that they can't understand everything other kids say. Or that they get overwhelmed by too much talking at all. The ways they cope may not always be – what you'd expect from your peers.'

I thought of the way I had run away from Sarah days before, how bizarre I'm sure it had looked. I think I understood what he meant.

'You mean they might act a little strange sometimes when they don't know what else to do?'

'That's exactly what I mean.' He beamed like I had answered a quiz question correctly. 'I just want you to know it's okay to feel a little out of place here at first. But remember that all the kids you meet today are like you under it all. They want to have fun. They want people to like them. They want friends.'

I nodded, not quite as afraid as I had been.

'Okay, let's go meet some kids.' He opened the door to one of the small rooms. This one looked pretty regular – a table, a whiteboard. A boy, who looked pretty ordinary, except maybe that he was a bit small, was sitting at the table with a teacher or assistant beside him.

'This is Josh. He won't say hello yet, but he'll be asking John, who's one of our aides, all about you when we leave.' Josh had put his head in his hands, but the adult with him gave a wave and a smile. I smiled back and gave Josh a little wave when he took a peek at me as we left to go to the room next door.

'This is Lilly.' Lilly was the opposite of Josh. She was up, out of her seat and standing nose to nose with me in a second.

'Who are you? How old are you?' She asked me, staring into my eyes. She made me a little nervous, but Mr Jenkins stepped in to help me out.

'Shall we give the poor girl a bit of space, Lilly?' he said, taking her arm and then introducing me.

'Show Jo the new app on your tablet,' her aide prompted. I spent the next ten minutes having a lesson from Lilly about her app to show people how she was feeling. Her fingers flew over the screen as she explained how it worked.

'It's because I don't always know how to say I'm mad,' she said. 'This helps me say it.'

'That's cool, Lilly,' I said, thinking that I could use something similar most of the time.

I continued to follow Mr Jenkins through a maze of small rooms, where he introduced me to kids and teachers and assistants at each stop, giving me a story for each that we met. I felt like some kind of visiting VIP being shown around.

It wasn't like school at all. There were still classes, but with only a few kids in each, or sometimes only one. Some of the rooms were for therapy, like learning to speak better, or exercises for the kids who had physical disabilities.

Despite meeting some pretty strange kids, I felt my muscles relaxing. Everyone had something they wanted to show me. Everyone seemed genuinely happy to see me. I was talking to more people here than I had talked to all year.

Then there was lunch, which was a little chaotic. Wheelchairs were jostled into places around two big tables. Some kids had hot lunches to be heated up. Things were spilled – and then cleaned up. Josh had to be led out when he started covering his ears and screaming. But there was lots of laughing too. I mostly just sat and watched it while I ate my sandwich. It was the first lunch hour I could remember when I didn't feel like everyone was watching *me*.

In fact at the end of lunch it took me a couple of tries to get Mr Jenkins's attention to lead me back through the maze to get out.

'Sure, sure,' he said, leaving a conversation he was having with someone, while also helping a student pack her lunch away.

Again I ran to catch up with him as we wound our way toward the entrance. Halfway there he stopped. This was the first time I had seen him stand still.

'Hey, you wouldn't happen to have Art in block H would you?'

'No, that's Science for me. Why?' I asked, wondering what this had to do with anything.

'Oh, nothing,' he dismissed. 'Just a crazy idea I had. Chris is in an art class that period and I'd love to get him some peer support instead of him having to drag his aide along with him all of the time.'

Thinking about Science, I remembered that between staying home on Friday and meeting Dr Sharon on Monday I had now missed two classes. Two classes of avoiding Sarah. All through the tour of the Special Education wing I had thought of her, though, wondering if she would find it as interesting as I did. Maybe I'd even tell her about it tomorrow. If it wasn't too late, and she was still talking to me.

'So, what do you think?' Mr Jenkins interrupted my thoughts. 'Are you up for meeting Chris still?'

'Sure, I guess so.'

'Great. We'll start on Monday then.'

That left me with three more lunch hours to survive in the main school. But then, maybe there was a chance it wouldn't be so bad. Even if it had to be only at school, maybe there was still hope for me to be friends with Sarah.

CHAPTER SEVEN

The next day went badly from the start. Grandma woke me up ridiculously early.

'Come now, Jo, up you get up for a proper breakfast.' It was 6:30 am and I didn't have to catch the school bus until 8:00 am. There was no arguing with Grandma though, no telling her that I *never* ate breakfast.

At least she was starting to let me take the school bus rather than driving me into town like she had the two days before, controlling my every second until school. Not that I loved the bus, filled as it was with kids I had gone to elementary school with, none of whom acknowledged that I was even alive. Still, I could ignore them too, pretending to be deeply involved in texting imaginary friends.

Today when I got on the bus, though, Lisa patted the seat beside her, inviting me to sit down.

'Where's Carmen?' I asked suspiciously.

Carmen and Lisa had been in my class since kindergarten and once upon a time we had all been sort-of friends. At least friends in the way that six- or seven-year-old girls are – playing on the playground, sharing 'secrets' and above all taking turns excluding one of the trio. Eventually I had been the permanently excluded one. There was the obvious reason of course – Lisa had once said *You're not my best friend anymore because my mom won't let a girl with a weird mom come to our house.*

But also, I had just never seemed to understand the rules of girl friendships. Who do you gossip about? What things do you say to sound cool? How do you tell when a compliment is actually meant to be an insult? These things had baffled me.

So I didn't think this invitation to sit with her could be good.

'She's sick I think,' Lisa dismissed, flicking her hair back with confidence and smiling widely.

'Oh,' was all that I could think to say.

'But anyway, how are you? I just don't see much of you now that we've moved onto bigger and better things.' We had seen each other most mornings for nearly a month since middle school started. We just hadn't spoken.

'Fine, I guess.' Keep it vague. Defences up.

Lisa's brow furrowed into a look of concern and she actually, the gall of her, smoothed my hair back with a mothering gesture.

'You're sure? My auntie saw an ambulance outside your house last week in the middle of the night. Nearly scared the pants off her. She knows we're friends and she was hoping you were okay.'

I felt my face flush deep red. Lisa's aunt lived two doors down from us. She had never, ever stepped foot in our house, invited us over to her house, or even so much as waved when she drove past us.

'No, I'm ok,' I managed.

The bus stopped, admitting another former classmate, Gorgeous George as he had secretly been called by the girls for the last couple of years. Lisa turned her sickly-sweet smile in his direction and used it to lure him into the seat behind us.

'How was the first basketball practice? The new uniforms are *so* cool!'

'Yup,' Gorgeous George articulately answered.

'Me and Carmen are going to go to every game – even the away ones. Our team is going to be the best with talent like you!'

I was never so glad to be so utterly ignored, as Lisa continued her hero-worship and George hung on her every word until they reached the school. As I got off the bus I put my hands into the pockets of my jacket. My left hand felt the pamphlet I had been handed on Monday. *Hi, I'm Chris.* The image of that boy floated from my pocket, juxtaposed with Ludicrous Lisa and Gorgeous George. There was nobody like *them* in the Special Education wing. It was hard to remember how good the day before had been though, when I had another day outside of it to face.

I spent all of first class worrying about seeing Sarah in science class second period. I couldn't help but repeatedly clench my stomach muscles, as I did when I got worried about something, and so by the end of the class I was starting to feel sick.

Would she bring up our awkward meeting last Thursday? Would she ask where I had been during the classes I'd missed? I imagined answering truthfully, *Well on Friday I stayed home because I was up all night when my mom had to go to the psychiatric ward. And then on Monday I missed class because I had to see a psychologist myself.* I could only hope she didn't ask.

I tried to make as late an entrance into science as I could without actually being late. I slipped into my seat just before the bell signalling the beginning of class. Unfortunately the teacher was still fiddling with his computer projector, trying to get the right slide on the screen, leaving far too much freedom for chat between classmates.

'Hi.' Sarah flashed me a quick, sincere smile that I couldn't help but return.

'Did I miss much?' I risked an idle comment.

'Well, no more flying body parts and Mr K put me with a partner who didn't have your surgery skills.'

I wished I didn't like Sarah so much. She was funny and kind and everything I wanted in a friend.

'Ah well, every operating theatre needs a few nurses too.'

I adopted a bad English accent and held out my hand with feigned dismissiveness. 'Scalpel please, Nurse Sheep-for-Brains.'

Sarah laughed openly. I didn't even know where that had come from. It had just fallen out of my brain. That is what happened when I talked to Sarah. So much for staying to myself.

When the end of class bell rang and I hurried to lose myself in the crowds spilling into the hallway, I found Sarah right behind me.

'Come to my locker. I've got a scarf for you that I found in a charity shop this weekend. It matches your purple top perfectly – so I couldn't resist.'

So I followed her. The image of Mom, arms bleeding, wailing, flashed through my mind and then disappeared.

Sarah was just opening her locker door when Lisa appeared.

'Hi again,' Lisa said.

I was about to respond when Sarah turned to Lisa with, 'Ahoy, locker mate. Hey, Lisa, do you know my friend Jo?' She turned to me.

Lisa gave me that sweet smile that promised every sort of underhanded nastiness. 'Of course I do. We go way back. Lots of good memories from old Elm Elementary.' I didn't know what shared memories Lisa was remembering, unless her favourite memories were of torture.

'Oh, good. Lisa and I are going to find out about the auditions for the play they're putting on in the spring. There's a meeting at lunch in the drama room for anyone interested. Want to go, Jo?'

What could I say with both of them smiling at me – one with open warmth, one with a malicious grin?

'Okay.'

There was just enough time for Sarah to plunk a bright striped scarf on top of my science books before the warning bell for third period rang and I headed for my locker to fetch my sketch pad for art.

As I walked into the drama room I scanned the small groups sitting together here and there. Sarah and Lisa were sitting in the back row of seats with their heads together in serious conversation. Sarah jerked upright when she saw me come in. She smiled, but it was a forced smile, seemingly for my benefit rather than coming from the heart. My heart started to pound. Something didn't feel right.

'There's poor Jo,' Lisa said with an overly-dramatic concerned smile as I approached.

'Why?' I asked suspiciously, but I was pretty sure now that I knew what Lisa was alluding to. So much for the new beginning. So much for any chance of having a real friend in Sarah.

Everyone in elementary school had known about my mom's coping problems. Right from my first day in school Mom had branded herself as bizarre. Instead of fussing over me, helping me to find my coat hook and passing comments with the other moms, she had left me standing shyly at the door to the kindergarten class and had marched over to the bookshelf. She had grabbed three books off the shelf and headed straight to the teacher with them.

'These have got to go,' she had stated, even though the teacher was kneeling down trying to coax a small boy to let go of his death grip on his mom's leg. I remember looking around and seeing that I was the only kid not standing with her mom. The teacher had stood up, confused.

'Pardon?'

I don't remember what exactly Mom said about the books – something about all the kids in the books having a mom and a dad, but whatever it was, it was loud enough to make everyone stop and look at her. It was the next thing she said that I remember most.

'She has no dad. There *is* no dad.' And she didn't just say it, she shouted it. The classroom had gone from noisy confusion to dead quiet in a second.

Mom – tall, with her curly hair springing around her head, her long floral skirt frayed on the bottom – had just stood there, not caring that everyone was staring at her, still holding out the books. For the first time I saw what everyone else saw. She didn't look like the other moms, she didn't talk like the other moms, she didn't act like the other moms and from the scared expressions on the kids' faces, and the way the moms pulled their kids closer, I could see that might not be a good thing.

After that, even if the kids had forgotten my mom's weird behaviour, their parents never stopped their vigilant lookout for craziness. Play dates with me were definitely discouraged. And that incident had happened when Mom was well.

I was pretty sure that Lisa had just shared some of these memorable times with Sarah, but I wasn't prepared for her next comment.

'Isn't Sarah a sweetheart, giving you that scarf? I've got lots of clothes I was sending off to charity if you want to come around to my house to look. We know how hard it is with your mom the way she is.' Lisa looked at Sarah conspiratorially. Sarah opened her mouth and then shut it without a word.

And I bolted. I just stood up, my lunch bag hit the ground, and I ran.

It was a long way home. My school was on the edge of the city about ten kilometres from the suburb we lived in. I could have waited for a city bus. There was a stop not too far from the school, but I just wanted to get away from the awfulness of the day as soon as possible. So instead I just kept running and walking until I came to my road and then I turned off down the little path to the river, the path to safety.

It was never going to change. I was never going to be known as 'Jo' without the attachment of 'with the crazy mother'. I expected this from Lisa. But it hurt a whole lot more to see Sarah gossiping about my mom. I'd let myself hope that she was different.

I should have been going straight home. I couldn't help but go to the cabin though. As soon as I opened the creaky, old door I felt better. I looked at my watch and it was only just before two. I could even start a small fire in the old fire-place and have an hour or so feeding sticks to the flames. With any luck I'd be able to show up at home on time and hope that the school hadn't phoned Grandma.

I put my hand in my pocket, searching for some paper to start the fire with. There was the pamphlet again. I brought it out and looked at it. *Hi, I'm Chris.*

I thought about the kids I had met the day before, about how they had all greeted me with big smiles. It was easy with them. It was too hard trying to fit in with kids like Lisa and Sarah. They were never going to let me forget that I couldn't fit in, would never fit in.

I decided right then that I would go back to Mr Jenkins and tell him I could start with Chris tomorrow. No more lunches in the main school. And – I was going to beg him to help get my timetable changed so that I had art with Chris instead of science in Block H. There had to be a way. I *never* wanted to see Sarah again.

CHAPTER EIGHT

The next morning I was back at the secretary's desk before the first bell. Luckily she connected me to Mr Jenkins before I lost my nerve. I didn't realise my hand was shaking until she passed me the phone.

'What can I do for you so early in the morning, Jo?' he asked.

'I was wondering if I could start coming today for lunch, instead of waiting until Monday.' I held my breath waiting for the answer.

'Don't see why not. Anything else?' He'd made it easier for me to ask the next question.

I let the breath out, remembering the words I had practised.

'Well, I was kind of wondering if there was a way I could get out of my science class so that I could go to Art with Chris.' I crossed my fingers that he didn't ask why.

He didn't.

'It might be a puzzle, but this early in the term I'm sure I could pull some strings,' he said. 'Chris will be delighted.'

In all of my thinking about never wanting to see Sarah

again, I had kind of forgotten about Chris. Now, back in the Special Education wing I felt nearly as nervous as I had the first day. What would Chris be like? What if he didn't like me? I'd kind of committed myself to spending a lot of time with him now.

Mr Jenkins had met me at the door again and as we walked he told me about Chris.

'Chris can't talk. We've tried a few systems to help him communicate, but nothing seems to work. He can't walk or control many of his movements. He has muscle spasms and occasionally he has epileptic seizures – we'll get you trained up to recognise these.' I wondered if there was anything he *could* do. I wasn't sure I was prepared for this. The kids I had met before seemed – not as complicated.

'We find that when he's in the lunch room with everyone he has a lot more difficulty eating, so we've been trying having him eat in a quiet room. But even on his own it may take him the whole fifty minutes to eat. We'll show you how to feed him.' Was this the 'teenage stuff' the pamphlet had talked about? I knew I was completely inept at fitting in with regular kids, but I was beginning to panic about what I was getting myself into with Chris.

Mr Jenkins must have seen my panic because he stopped and pointed to a picture on a bulletin board. Unlike the rapid spiel he had started with, his next words were quiet and measured.

'This is Chris at a baseball game last year.' There was the same boy from the pamphlet, with a cap on and that same lopsided grin. 'My eighteen year old son helped us out on that field trip and spent most of the time assisting Chris. It was the first time I'd really seen him smile.'

I just looked at him. What did this have to do with me?

'It may be a lot about helping Chris with things he can't do, but what you can *certainly* do, that I can't, is make him smile. Believe me, I've tried.'

Still I felt confused.

'How? What can I do?'

'Nothing special. Just be a normal enough kid and talk to him. For some reason that's the key to Chris's smile.'

So I didn't run away, though my heart was pounding fast when we came to the room Chris was waiting in.

'Chris, Jo. Jo, Chris. And Florence, Chris's aide.' Mr Jenkins had resumed his whirlwind pace. 'Florence will show you the how to of lunch with Chris and then she is heading back to me to help out with Amanda. 'All right, Flo?'

And he was off.

The boy in front of me was in an enormous wheelchair. It seemed to take up most of the small room we were in. His head was cradled in what looked like a semi-halo of blue neoprene. There was an equally blue bar holding back each of his shoulders and a belt that strapped in his chest. The whole contraption was somehow tilted back so that he

69

looked like he was in a big reclining chair. With all of the restraining bits, his arms and legs were still free and all four of them were flailing wildly.

'He's a bit excited to see you, aren't you, Chris?' Florence almost cooed the last part, as if talking to a baby in a high-chair. 'Watch out for this one, he likes the girls. You still have to eat your lunch though. There's a good boy.'

I had never felt so self-conscious in my life. I didn't know what to say. I didn't know how to say anything. Mr Jenkins had said I only needed to talk to him. I didn't know if I could talk like this.

'Hi, Chris.' Surely I couldn't go wrong with greeting him. I sat down in the empty chair at the table.

'Ok, Chris. Let's show Jo how you eat, ok? And no funny stuff today!'

Chris had a big terry towel bib on. Florence had what looked like a big baby spoon in one hand and a tea towel in the other. Chris's limbs had settled down, but when Florence raised the spoon to his mouth they started up again and she had to manoeuvre the spoon around an arm into Chris's open mouth. It didn't all make it in and with the tea towel she wiped away the bits that ended up on his lips. My eyes travelled to the dish of food in front of the aide. Some sort of stew, I guessed. It too was in a bowl more fitting for a toddler.

I hadn't asked Mr Jenkins any questions and now suddenly I had some, but I didn't think I should ask them in front of

Chris. Could he understand me? Was he like a giant baby or was his brain ok? What should I talk about?

After two more spoonfuls of food, intermittent with, 'there's a good boy' and 'good eating, Chris!' Florence handed me the spoon. I half expected to hear 'go on, there's a good girl!' but Florence's voice returned to a normal intonation.

'It's that simple. Just dodge Chris's limbs if you can. Don't worry though, sometimes you can't and we've all had to clean some food off the walls from time to time!'

I took the spoon and tried to follow the way Florence had fed Chris. My movements felt far too tentative and awkward though. I was sitting too far away and couldn't reach around Chris's tense arm that jutted toward me. After two attempts I stood up and managed to get most of a spoonful of mush into his mouth and then gingerly wiped the rest away with the towel, trying to avoid touching the boy's arm.

'Good. You've got the jig of it,' Florence said. 'Ok, Chris. Can I trust you with this young girl?'

I felt my cheeks burn with embarrassment – more for Chris than for me. I just wanted the aide to leave. I felt I wouldn't be so self-conscious in feeding Chris. And I wouldn't have to talk in this sickly sweet way that felt so . . . wrong.

When the aide left, the boy looked at me with that big smile I had seen in all the photos.

'I don't know that I'm so good at this,' I said, half to myself.

I thought of the alternative – hiding from Sarah and Lisa,

feeling sick and mortified.

'I'll try though.'

I was silent as I somehow got most of the food into Chris over the next twenty minutes. In that quietness the boy's limbs gradually slowed down. I gave him the last spoonful and sat down, looking at my watch. Still ten minutes until the end of lunch and there was no sign of anyone coming back.

'So,' I said. 'Did Mr Jenkins tell you my name was Jo?'

I remembered that he had. Another stupid thing to say – if he even knew what I was saying.

I looked at the boy. He didn't smile again, but his eyes were meeting mine.

I realised that this was the first time I had properly looked at him. I'd spent the whole time concentrating on the job of getting food into him, and somehow not seeing him. Mr Jenkins really had to think harder about the photos he used in his pamphlets, because instead of the geeky hair and clothes I'd expected, Chris's jeans and trainers were both brands everyone wore and his hair was pretty normal too.

He looked at me again expectantly.

'I'm hiding out here you know.' It just slipped out. 'I hope you don't mind. I mean, you might be expecting someone fun and normal. But I'm a bit of a screw up.'

I sat for another minute, not sure what I should say in the silence.

'I don't have any friends. I don't even know how to have friends. My mom isn't exactly a role model in normalness. And the worst part is, everyone knows it. She doesn't care if she's weird. And I don't really either, most of the time. But everyone else does, and they're afraid I'm as weird as her. I thought it would be different this year. I got all the right clothes. I take the bus to school, so nobody needs to know about my mom. But it doesn't matter.' For some reason it seemed easy to just keep talking.

'But you know, I guess that's for the best. I kind of have enough to do at home. See, my mom isn't just weird. She's on medications and stuff.'

I looked over again. The boy was completely quiet – no movement. And his eyes were firmly on mine. Was he listening? I felt like I was truly seeing him now, not just his wheelchair. He had these incredibly deep brown eyes and his stare was intense, like he was listening like nobody had ever listened to me before. It wasn't exactly like the wheelchair and his body all at weird angles disappeared; I was still pretty uncomfortable with him. But his eyes kind of opened a window to who he was under all of that. Chris, this was Chris.

CHAPTER NINE

I walked into the hospital lounge with twice the confidence I had the last time. It felt like it was a month since I had been here instead of only a week ago. I wasn't afraid of this hospital wing anymore. I'd seen stranger over the last week in the special education wing and I was starting to feel comfortable with it.

It was going to be good to see Mom. I needed to get away from Grandma. In the last week and a half I had been given almost no choice in any aspect of my life. It didn't feel like a break from the responsibility of watching out for Mom anymore. It was more like being treated like I wasn't capable of even watching out for myself.

Instead of feeling like I was being taken care of in a special way, a motherly way that my own mother could never quite achieve, I was feeling imprisoned. Besides, I wasn't a kid anymore.

But Grandma was still treating me like one and it was getting harder to be the kid that she expected me to be. This morning was the perfect example. I had wandered into the kitchen at 10a.m., surprised that I had been allowed to sleep in. Lined up on the kitchen table were piles of clothes. As usual, Grandma was busy in the kitchen, head in the oven, rear end stuck up in the air.

'Morning,' I had mumbled as I opened the cupboard looking for some sugar-coated cereal before yet another bowl of porridge was plunked down in front of me.

'A bit of a treat for you on the table, Jo,' Grandma had stated, while she carried on with her kitchen work. That was her way. She presented criticism or disappointment in the same matter of fact manner as a compliment, or this – a present.

I had approached the present tentatively. I wasn't sure what I would find, but I didn't think it could be good. There were four complete outfits compiled on the table in four separate, impossibly straight piles. I had picked up each item and tried to carefully lay them back as neatly as they had been.

To be fair to Grandma the clothes weren't awful. It was more that each outfit matched so exactly and they were just that slightly bit out of style that anyone would notice because they were so new. Plus everything was either frilly or a cut and material that demanded to be crease free. I knew that there would be no getting out of wearing them though.

'Thanks, Grandma.' I had tried to sound excited, but my voice had come out too high and too flat. If Grandma had noticed, and I was pretty sure she had, she hadn't shown it.

'Get a move on then. We've a half hour drive to the hospital and it won't do to be late.'

So here I was, in the least uncomfortable, least glaringly out-of-date outfit. In retrospect I thought I should have chosen the worst, as nobody here would notice or care what I was wearing. Tomorrow I would have a tougher decision as to which I would have to wear to school.

An hour of escape from Grandma wasn't the only reason I wanted to see my mom though. I wanted to tell her about my week. Not the bad, beginning bit. I never told her how bad school usually was for me. Mom had enough bad to deal with without taking on my problems too. I wanted to tell her about Chris.

She wasn't sitting in the familiar green plastic chair this week though. Today she was standing right under the television that was perched near the ceiling in the corner. She was staring intensely at it, watching some sort of news show.

When I touched her arm in greeting, Mom never took her eyes from the screen. She shook my touch off as if it were an annoying fly.

'See that?' she shouted, pointing vehemently at the screen. 'They're at it again. Attacking people's right to knowledge!'

'Hi, Mom.' I tried again to connect with her. 'I'm really glad to see you.'

I wanted to be able to hug her, to recapture that warm embrace we had shared the week before. Here was the mom I knew though – not the pretend mom I had somehow convinced myself I would meet. This mom didn't give out hugs lightly.

She was gearing up for a rant. I could tell. She always was when the finger started pointing. If I could only shift the focus, maybe she would be interested enough to listen to me today.

'Mom, you've been saying for ages that I need a passion. I think I've found one!'

I thought back to my last week in the special education wing and with Chris. Mr Jenkins *had* arranged for me to switch my art class to Chris's art class so I could help him there. It hadn't been that difficult; Mr Jenkins would teach me science in the block my art used to be in. I couldn't believe it could be this easy to escape my life!

The knot that was always in my stomach from the moment I walked in the metal school door was beginning to loosen. I found myself almost looking forward to my time in the special education wing.

It hadn't taken much more than a few minutes for me to figure out that school was entirely different in the special education wing. For one, the bells didn't sound in this wing, so the teachers didn't necessarily know that the class was supposed to start – and they didn't seem to care. I'd waited more than ten minutes in the classroom Mr Jenkins had told me to go to for science before he finally showed up. I had almost thought I was in the wrong room. When he finally did arrive, it was to sit down in front of me, no plan, and ask, 'So where are you at in science anyway?'

'Um – well. We just dissected an eye?' That was pretty much what I remembered.

'Ok. Biology. We can cover that pretty quickly. I'll look at it for next class. We can afford to skip this one. There's a class going on that could use your help.'

I had never met a teacher like this. He didn't have that invisible line of authority that all teachers took everywhere.

So instead of learning science that period, I had helped Lilly measure out her ingredients for chocolate brownies. According to Mr Jenkins it was a math class – measurement.

The first thing she had said to me was, 'I like you, Jo. I won't pinch you, ok?'

Maybe it wasn't the most normal thing for someone to say, but the message behind it made me feel good. None of us was exactly normal, but it didn't matter. There was no one I had to impress here, no worries of saying something that would reveal me as odd or uncool. Just this freedom to ... be.

I thought Mom would like to hear about this hidden part of school. She would like Mr Jenkins, I just knew it. She would like that he didn't seem to follow any rules – just like her. One of her favourite topics was about how teachers were so caught up in teaching rules, conformity Mom called it, that they didn't have time to teach anything interesting or important.

But my heart sank when her only response to my excitement was, 'Passion. That's what they're killing now!'

The channel on the television had been changed – to the same murder mystery show that Mom and I had watched last week. Unfortunately, it didn't seem to settle her at all.

'Higher fees again! Jo, you won't be able to go to university at this rate!' At least she had finally acknowledged my existence.

'But do you see anyone taking to the streets? No passion for it. I need to be out there stirring up the passion.' Mom's arms were in motion now – big arcs to emphasise just how 'out there' she already was.

I suddenly felt utterly alone. I walked over and sat in one of the green chairs, leaving her to her audience-less performance. So much for sharing things with her. I actually missed Chris now. Chris, the out of the ordinary boy who I'd now spent two lunch hours and an art class with.

At least he smiled every time I met him. And I could talk to him. I didn't know what he understood yet, but at least he seemed more interested in me than my own mother.

By our second lunch hour together we had settled into a bit of a routine. Chris smiled his huge, trademark smile when I came in, and for the first few minutes his excited limbs filled the small room. I'd learned to wait until he settled again before we started to eat.

Then I had to concentrate a bit to make sure that I actually got some food into Chris without impaling him with the spoon and with keeping the place reasonably food free. Then I'd take all of the dishes and laundry to the little kitchen where the special meals were heated up and the special dishes and laundry washed.

That usually left us with ten or fifteen minutes before the end of lunch. For some reason I couldn't help myself from rambling on and on. It wasn't even like I was filling uncomfortable silence anymore either. I'd learned that being quiet while Chris ate helped him to stay still. I was okay with that quiet.

It was more that he looked at me expectantly when we had that time left at the end of lunch, and it made me just talk.

'Well, you know how I told you about the thing with Lisa and Sarah?' Chris had given me a bit of a grin at that. I didn't know if it was just the sound of my voice that he liked or what. The way Florence talked to Chris, it seemed he couldn't understand much. But he seemed happy, so I just kept talking.

'I still have to take the bus with Lisa, but it's like the other day never, ever happened. She doesn't even look in my direction when I get on the bus. I don't know what that means. Do you?' I had looked at Chris, hoping that he magically had some insight into the intricacies of social interaction that I lacked. He'd raised his eyebrows, but I couldn't be sure that was a movement he meant to make.

'I'm more afraid to run into Sarah. I thought she was interested in being my friend, not just curious about my mom ...'

It felt strangely good to talk to Chris. These were thoughts that I usually pushed to the back of my brain and here they were tumbling out of my mouth.

I sat in the hospital chair and tried to blink back my tears of disappointment. One of the nurses behind the glassed in counter came out and pulled another chair beside me. She took my hand and gave it a squeeze.

'It can be a bit frightening when your mom isn't well, can't it?'

I opened my mouth to dispute this. I wasn't scared. I was sad. Nothing to do with Mom being unwell, just sadness about Mom being the way she was all the time, and wishing that she was different somehow. I wished that she could, just once in a while, look at me like Chris did when I started to talk. I wished that she wanted to know how I felt and what I thought. I closed my mouth without voicing this though. What was the point? It was never going to change.

CHAPTER TEN

'So, I went to see my mom yesterday, Chris.' We were halfway through his bowl of diced up pasta, and it was a good eating day. It wasn't taking too much of my concentration to make the target, so I could talk at the same time as feeding him.

'It didn't go well. I love her and all, but sometimes I just wish I could wake up one day and she'd be normal, all better.' I felt a little guilty for this emerging pattern of long monologues at lunch. Maybe I was more similar to Mom than I thought. Chris didn't seem to mind though. At least he was stiller when I talked on and on.

'It isn't even like she has this real mental illness. If she was schizophrenic or bipolar I could at least say that to people. I got this pamphlet once about teaching people not to be afraid of mental illness. Basically it said if people took their medication they were like everyone else.' Chris was watching me intently.

'It made me laugh. That's not my mom. She's so screwed up she's had all the labels for a time and none of them stuck. Now it's just "non specific psychiatric illness",' I continued.

'And do you know what that means, Chris? It means 'we haven't got a clue and we don't know how to fix it'.'

Chris flashed me his trademark lopsided grin and one leg spasmed in an enthusiastic kick. Maybe it was wishful thinking, but I could swear he had a sense of humour and found my description quite funny.

I finally asked Mr Jenkins how much Chris understood. I caught him in the hallway as I headed to see Dr Sharon after helping Chris with his lunch.

'Can I ask you a question?' I was feeling less and less shy with the adults in the SE, as everyone here seemed to abbreviate the wing.

'Fire away.' He was carrying an armful of dirty bibs and towels. The SE even had its own washing machine. So much of this part of the school was about everything other than learning.

'What does Chris understand? Is he, like, retarded?' I knew this probably wasn't the politically correct term. Just like 'crazy' was never supposed to be used; it was 'psychiatric illness', as if using different words wiped the craziness clean away.

'His label, Jo? Everyone has one here, and reams of reports dating all the way back to when they were born.' Mr Jenkins tried to move on but I stood still, waiting for the answer.

'Chris's label is Cerebral Palsy. He didn't get enough oxygen when he was being born. It affected every part of him profoundly, including his brain.'

'Does that mean he can't understand anything I say?'

'Does it matter? He's happy with you, Jo. You just keep doing what you're doing, and Chris's sweet personality will keep shining through. We don't value people on the basis of their IQ around here.'

I wasn't sure if it mattered or not. It wasn't that I thought less of him if he wasn't able to understand much, and Mr Jenkins had as much as said he couldn't. It was just that I found myself telling Chris things that I never told anyone. Mostly it was *because* I didn't think Chris understood much that I felt that I could talk to him. But there was a small part of me that longed for him to be the friend that finally understood me.

* * *

It seemed that Mondays were going to be Dr Sharon days. Only the time was different from the last week.

I arrived into Dr Sharon's empty little room fresh from lunch with Chris, happy to be missing P.E., but not sure what I was going to talk about.

'So?' Dr Sharon asked, her stillness so starkly opposite to Chris's movement, yet almost equally silent. Why was it so much easier to fill the silence with words when I was with Chris now, and yet not have a single word to speak to this counsellor, when the whole point was to talk?

'Well,' I started tentatively, 'thanks for making that lunch time thing happen.'

Dr Sharon smiled.

'It sounds as if it were you that made that happen.'

I couldn't disagree. In this one area of my life I felt in control of something for the first time ever. *I* could make Chris smile. *I* was guiding his hand to create abstract paintings. *I* had conquered my fears of something new and that was leading to this new feeling of belonging, or at least the beginning of it.

'I guess so,' I agreed. 'The funny thing is, I think I'd want to help Chris even if I wasn't there just because. . .'

I shrugged. I didn't want to talk to Dr Sharon about my trouble with practically everything. I had to admit that she had taken me seriously *and* she had been able to help me. I felt I probably could trust her, and she just may help me in more ways. Still, it wasn't easy for me to share how I felt about anything in my life. I just wasn't used to talking to people about anything that was real, or important or true.

So I used the forty-five minutes to talk about how much I was enjoying working with Chris. But then, I suppose that this *was* real, and important, and true.

* * *

The next morning Grandma and I had our first ever fight. It was over the clothes of course.

On Monday I had dutifully worn the corduroy pants and blouse she had given me. The last two yet-to-be-worn outfits included skirts, and I just couldn't make myself put on either. I had always felt so awkward wearing any kind of dress or skirt, and Mom of course had never made me wear one.

Instead, I slipped on my most comfortable pair of jeans and the cool t-shirt I had excitedly purchased in the summer, knowing it was exactly in style.

I noticed the usual bowl of porridge and a cup of tea when I walked into the kitchen. Grandma was already sitting down drinking her own cup of tea. I sighed.

'To do good to the ungrateful is to throw rose-water into the sea, I notice,' Grandma quoted.

'It's just, I don't even eat breakfast before school.'

'That's when your mother is here. We eat breakfast together.' Every bit of life with Grandma had to be her way. No negotiation.

'Oh.' I could never find the courage to disagree with my solid, stoic grandmother.

'I mean the clothes of course, Jo. I thought you'd appreciate some new things. God knows your mother never finds it in herself to buy any.'

'Can't you EVER say anything nice about her?!' I exploded. Anger shot through me and I couldn't help but let it erupt.

She looked shocked for a second and then regained her

usual neutral expression. I had *never* raised my voice to her before.

'Well! It is certainly not a good morning.' She stood up, taking my untouched bowl of porridge to the sink.

As quickly as I had felt infuriated, my anger turned to guilt. After all, Grandma was only doing her best and didn't mean to buy me clothes that were horrible. She had left the room quickly though, and I was afraid to follow her to apologise. I was afraid the anger I had felt was too close to the surface still to trust that I could contain it.

CHAPTER ELEVEN

Three days a week Chris and I went to Art together. We were on our own in a completely different culture when we left the safety of the SE wing.

It was tricky to push Chris's chair through the hallways and to manoeuvre through doorways that seemed too narrow for his big chair. I was afraid that I might tip the chair over and then what would I do?

Plus, I felt that people were staring at us, or trying hard not to look at us. While I had never felt like I fit in, at least the sight of me didn't scare kids off like Chris in his big blue contraption did. I wondered if he noticed how almost everyone avoided coming too near him. Or was he used to it because he had never known any different? I wished I could ask him how he felt.

I was learning a lot about Chris in art. He was so different as soon as I wheeled him into the art room. He didn't smile, keeping his eyes on the paints that I put on the high table. He didn't look at me at all either. His whole focus was on the task at hand.

His limbs became less stiff when I put a paintbrush in

his hand. I tried to release any of my own thoughts when I supported him to paint. It was freeing, because all of me disappeared and I was just facilitating his creativity, at least I thought I might be. It was still me that led his hand to the red or the blue. But I was learning that in subtle ways he did make his own decisions. If I paid attention to the tension in his arm I would know what colour he might be choosing. Go toward the green, resistance. Go toward the yellow, his arm moved easily that way. But it was guessing, and I found that as soon as I started questioning myself I was less certain that Chris was telling me anything.

We worked in the corner of the art room, where there was a table that could be adjusted to fit over Chris's wheelchair. Everyone else sat at two long tables. Mr Jenkins had said that this was an 'integrated' class for Chris, and with me assisting him it might mean that kids would interact more with him than if Florence was with him. It didn't seem like I was going to make any difference though.

The kids in this class were in the grade above me and even though I'd gone to elementary school with many of them, not one of them had ever said hello to me this year. And they didn't now. In fact they didn't even look at me or Chris. It was as if we were invisible. And yet I just knew by the way they whispered to each other that we definitely weren't. I glanced at Chris to see if he felt as out of place as I did, but if he did he didn't show it.

At least the rest of the class was painting too, but that's where the similarities ended. Everyone else was working on copying a print of a famous artist of their choosing. Chris didn't have a print to copy.

The teacher didn't come around to him either. The week before he had pointed out Chris's cupboard. No one else had a cupboard.

'This is where Chris's art materials are kept. You can ask me for more if you run out.' This had been directed at me, with no interaction with him. While Florence might be too babying with him, I thought it was probably better than ignoring him completely. I didn't see how this was teaching, or how I was going to get credit for what I was doing.

I talked quietly to Chris; imaging that he had a plan for his painting.

'Ok. Blue is good. It looks quite calming so far. Should we go with a bit of complimentary colour?' I guided his hand toward the green paint on the pallet, but felt his arm stiffen, before a spasm gripped it, resulting in a wide strip of blue paint down my cheek. If I had been in the SE, I probably would have laughed, but two boys at the nearest table chuckled instead. I wiped the paint away, without looking at them and without even smiling. It wasn't funny anymore.

'Okay. You show me then. Which colour?' I moved his arm slowly, feeling for where he might want it to stop. Orange. He gripped the paint brush tightly and moved his arm himself to deliver a thick circle of paint to the corner of his paper. This was another difference. All of the other kids were painting on canvas. Not Chris. He got primary school paper.

I supposed the two paintings I had helped him to paint didn't look like much. They certainly could be primary school paintings. Still, they didn't seem to just be random swipes of paint. Each was quite different from the other. Different colours, different brush strokes. And I had learned straight away that Chris was not happy to have a paper taken before it was fully covered in paint.

During our first class I had taken away the paper after it was covered with a few strokes, thinking that it was getting a bit messy, and I could just keep giving him new papers to do a few brush strokes on. He had flailed wildly and I had not been able to guide his hand to any paint. After a few minutes of attempting, I had taken the brush from him, thinking he was tired of painting. He had then swept the second paper off the table with his better arm.

The first painting was just out of his reach on the table, but while I had washed out brushes at the sink, Chris had jerked and rocked toward it until he could trap a corner of the paper under his hand. When I returned, he was sitting as still as he could, the corner firmly under his knuckles. I had sat down, unsure of how to fill the rest of the time if he didn't seem to want to paint.

'What now?' I had asked quietly. Chris had frowned at me

and then down at the paper. And then he had done it again. And again.

When I had moved the painting in front of him his eyes stayed firmly on the paper. So I'd brought back the paints. He'd given me a triumphant smile and sure enough had continued to paint. This time I had let him tell me when he was finished.

* * *

Mr Jenkins and I were falling into a rhythm for science.

'Ok. So, parts of the eye. Here's the diagram.' He placed a labelled picture in front of me. 'You'll need to be able to label all of the parts for the test.'

'Right. Got it.' I wrote *Parts of the eye* under my *for the next test* heading.

'Next. Assignment of the day. Page 38. Five questions there about what the parts of the eye do. That's your work for the day. Page 30 to 37 will give you the answers.'

'Ok. Got it.'

'Now, do you have a particular interest in how the eye works? Burning questions? If you do, now's the time. Let's talk science.'

'Not really. Don't think optometry is for me.' I could pretty much say anything in this class.

'Okay then. You work away and meet me in the resource room when you're done.'

I'd quickly finish up my work and then spend the rest of the class helping Mr Jenkins with whatever was needed. Sometimes it was folding laundry, sometimes it was reading with one of the kids. Every day was different in the Special Education wing. And I loved it.

* * *

The next two weeks seemed to fly by. There was something to look forward to at school every day. Even on the one day a week with no art or science, I had lunch with Chris. So between school and hiding out at my cabin as much as I could get away with, life with Grandma was even falling into a tolerable rhythm.

'It was a pretty nice day, wasn't it, Grandma?'

'A fine day. I put the washing out on the line and it was dry in less than two hours.'

After the awful day at the hospital, things began to improve with Mom as well. She was on a new drug, and by the next visit she actually seemed almost normal. She was even allowed to go out and we had walked down to the park and fed the ducks the cupcakes Mom bought on the way.

'Every duck needs a real treat once in a while,' she had rationalised. Ok, so she was never going to be completely normal, but feeding cupcakes to ducks on a sunny afternoon was a huge step up from ranting to herself.

Now we were talking on the phone every evening. And

most nights Mom showed at least a slight interest in me before she went off on a tangent about herself.

'So, tell me what you read today, Jo.'

'Well, I looked on your shelf and found *Watership Down* and I used to love that book when you read it to me, so I thought I'd read it myself.'

'Excellent choice, my sentimental penguin, you.'

I smiled. It felt good to hear a new pet name. It was a good sign.

'I'm writing you a list of "Must Reads" before you turn sixteen. It's a watershed age and some books you've got to read before you're too cynical to stop appreciating them. I'm thinking that I might look into teaching a community course on children's literature. There is such a dearth of knowledge as to the true children's classics.'

My typical self-centred mother. This time, when she came home though, I was going to do everything I could to help her keep happy, if it meant having these sorts of conversations every minute we were together.

CHAPTER TWELVE

Chris was driving me crazy. I had gotten used to his sudden jerks and random flailing limbs, and most of the time I could dodge his arms and legs when I was helping him with lunch or art. In the last week though, it seemed to be so much worse. I was going home with bruised shins from the kicks.

'Ok. One more spoonful and we're done here.' He booted me again as I raised the spoon to hopefully be done with his dinner. 'Ouch, Chris! That hurt!'

I was trying to be patient. Mr Jenkins had said that Chris didn't have control of these movements, so it wasn't that he meant to kick me. But something was wrong.

I had come to see that I could influence Chris's spasms. If I was very calm, or if I talked in a steady voice to him, or if we were in a quiet space Chris became stiller. Art worked for him too. When his eyes were on what he was painting, he seemed to have so much more control over his arms and hands.

It was usually when he seemed excited, or if there was a lot going on around him, that Chris lost control and I knew

I would have to dodge his limbs.

This week, though, even when we were in our quiet lunch room and even when Chris seemed to be as in control as possible, these random kicks came out of nowhere.

It was beginning to grate on my nerves, especially on days when I came to school already tense from trying to keep my temper with Grandma. This was supposed to be my sanctuary.

I tried again to get the last spoonful of food into Chris's mouth and yet again his right foot collided with my shin. I cursed my bad reflexes, *knowing* that kick had been coming. Knowing the kick had been coming ... There was a pattern!

Then I thought back to my first day of painting with Chris, and the way he had used his body to get across the message that *he* would tell *me* when he was done with a painting. He was communicating! These weren't random kicks; they were a message to me. I was sure of it.

'Chris, you don't like this, do you?'

Chris gave me the biggest grin.

His food never looked very appealing. Florence had explained that Chris's swallowing reflex was pretty poor, so he could only eat foods that were nearly mush. Still, usually the mush was a slightly different colour each day and I could often tell by the smell what it had been before being made into mush.

I looked down at the last spoonful from this bowl. I hadn't

noticed until now that it had been the same food all week. It was Thursday now. It had *definitely* been in the last week that the kicking had started.

* * *

For once, I wanted to see Grandma as soon as I got home.

'Please, please can you make shepherd's pie for dinner?'

'I haven't any lamb, Jo,' she said.

'It can be with mince beef,' I begged, uncharacteristically throwing my arms around her thick middle. 'A big pan of it. We need leftovers. I promised a friend at school a taste of your famous shepherd's pie. He's never had a proper one.'

Grandma remained stiff, and her expression never changed, but she sighed in acquiescence.

'Don't take off your shoes then. Get yourself in the car.' I thought I saw a hint of a smile. 'Since you've promised the original, I'll have to get the lamb. No point in using the wrong ingredients.'

I couldn't wait until lunch the next day. I had packed a big container of Grandma's best shepherd's pie, enough for me and Chris. Grandma had gone all out and also made soda bread with real buttermilk as well, and I had kept quiet about the fact that Chris probably wouldn't be able to eat that.

I had thought about lunch hours with Chris. There were days when it was easier to feed him. Sure, there were always those involuntary missiles of arms and legs to be avoided. But some days he seemed to fight to keep them under control and to get his head into a position that made it easier to get the spoon to his mouth.

Why were some days easier than others? I thought it must have to do with what he was eating. How much choice in what he ate, or anything, did he have? Of course, everyone in the SE did their best to make Chris smile, but had anyone ever directly asked him anything? And what about at home? I didn't even know anything about his home. I had been so busy talking about my own life; I hadn't thought to find out anything about Chris's.

I asked to use the microwave to heat up the meal. I hoped that I had guessed right about what he would most want to eat. Hopefully my memory was right in leading me to think that mashed potatoes and mashed up meat seemed to be a favourite. Shepherd's pie was the one thing I could think of that would have the right consistency not to choke Chris, without having to put it in a blender to turn to unappealing goo.

'Ok, Chris,' I said as I walked in, putting the plate of food in front of him. I had also snuck out one of Mom's pottery plates, the brightest one of the mismatched pile. If Chris was going to have nice food, I wanted it to be on a proper plate. 'I'm listening. Or at least, I'm trying to listen.'

I looked at him and smiled. He grinned back at me. His arms and legs thrashed, but I just waited patiently until they settled down again.

'This is my grandma's famous dish. I don't know anyone who doesn't like it. But let me know if you don't. I'm listening,' I reiterated.

Chris did seem to like it, or at least I wasn't receiving the thumping I had endured all week.

Florence had also delivered Chris's lunch in his usual preschool-style bowl. It was the same meal that he had had all week. I suddenly thought to see what he would do if I switched to this meal.

'Trust me! Tell me if I'm right in hearing that you don't like this mush,' I said as I raised a spoonful to his mouth. Sure enough, his right leg darted out and I moved back just in time to avoid another bruise.

My stomach fluttered in excitement. Chris was talking to me! He really was! This kick meant something. He was saying *NO* in the one way he could.

I was quiet as we finished the lunch. Chris's body was quiet too. I didn't know what he was thinking about, but my mind was whirling with questions to ask him – questions that I was pretty sure he could answer no to.

* * *

Last period of the day on Fridays was my new science block. I was doing my work as fast as I could, bursting to tell Mr Jenkins of my breakthrough with Chris and to ask him the questions that I had been starting to wonder about.

'Slow it down, Jo!' Mr Jenkins said, as he swept back into the room after stepping out to help one of the aides who had requested help with a transfer. One of the wheelchair users needed to lie down after a seizure. I now knew that the big machine with bits hanging off it that I had seen on the first day in the SE was called a hoist, and it was used to move kids from wheelchairs to other chairs or to the floor.

'*You* can talk. You're always rushing about yourself,' I found myself secure enough to retort in jest.

'Guilty,' he said holding up his hands and straddling the chair opposite my table. 'Really, though, what's the rush today?'

I told him all about my week with Chris and how I was certain he was trying very deliberately to communicate with me. Mr Jenkins listened as I spoke, nodding his head and not interrupting me. When I was finished, he just sat quietly a moment, looking down. When he looked up I was sure that I wasn't going to like what he had to say next.

'Listen, Jo. I don't want to dash your enthusiasm, I really don't,' he said. 'I totally agree that Chris is letting you know when he doesn't like his food. You know as well as I do by now that he obviously has likes and dislikes.'

'But?'

'But I don't want you to be disappointed if he isn't able to understand words you say to him.'

'Have you ever actually asked him anything?' I was annoyed that Mr Jenkins, who I thought would understand how important this was, didn't seem to get it at all. 'I'm not expecting that we'll be discussing Shakespeare or anything! I just think that Chris has *something* to say.'

'And he does say it, in his own way, all of the time.'

I no longer wanted to ask Mr Jenkins any of the questions I had come to class hoping to get answered. I'd ask Chris himself. Somehow I would find a way to ask him the questions nobody else was bothering to ask.

CHAPTER THIRTEEN

Mom was coming home! It seemed much longer than just over five weeks that she had been in the hospital. So much had changed for me.

Nothing had apparently changed between Grandma and Mom though. During the whole time Mom was in the hospital, Grandma had never visited her once and they had not even spoken on the phone. It was always me who ran for the phone when it rang in the evenings at the time when Mom always made her phone call. Grandma would suddenly be very busy somewhere in the furthest part of the house from the phone.

It wasn't that she didn't care at all; I knew that. She talked to the social worker at least a couple of times a week, and I had overheard parts of a few of these conversations.

'Is she getting on all right? Does she need anything?' she had asked, gripping the phone tightly, when Mom had first been in the hospital.

'I might send her in a few more bits of comfortable clothing,' she had suggested later in the month.

'Tell me, now, is she still going to that group thing you

mentioned?' she had inquired, obviously being kept informed, when Mom had started to finally improve.

'Do you think this new medication is going to work?' she had asked, eyes shining with hope, just last week.

But it was me who went in to help Mom carry her two bags when we collected her on a Saturday afternoon.

The drive home was quiet. With Mom reading a book in the front seat of the car, and Grandma only occasionally asking if everyone was warm enough, it would have been difficult for anyone observing to even believe we all knew each other.

* * *

On Monday, I was ready with my questions for Chris, and I had a new idea of how he might answer them. If it worked, I would be able to prove that he wasn't just vaguely showing his unhappiness with his kicks.

I had spent Sunday helping Grandma make meals for the freezer. I had asked her if she could cook us a few things to save, before she drove home on Monday. I had told her it would be handy for days when both Mom and I were out until later. Mom had raised her head from her book suspiciously at the request, but said nothing.

I had leftover chicken dinner for Chris today. I'd had to use the blender for the meat, but the mashed carrots and turnips, the mashed potatoes, and the chicken were all on their own corner of the plate, not the usual grey mass all together. But while I hoped that he liked the dinner, I was way more excited about the bit of time we might have after the dinner was over.

'So, my mom came home and I think she's much better. It's hard to tell because she won't stop reading until Grandma leaves. I think it's her way of not yelling at her.'

It was definitely a good eating day. There was hardly a jerk from him.

'It's weird, having her home. I didn't think about her as much this time. Usually I worry, worry, worry the whole time she is in hospital.'

Another two bites for Chris and I took a couple of hurried bites of my own sandwich.

'Plus, I was thinking, when she went into the hospital I was in bits about trying to be her daughter *and* have friends. And now I don't even care about friends,' I thought out loud, and then added, 'Well, there's you of course, Chris. But it doesn't count to my mom. She's only worried if I have a life outside school and home – and this is just school to her.'

We were both finished our lunches in record time. I glanced at my watch. Twenty minutes left.

I put the dishes to the side and sat down opposite to Chris. Out of my bag I brought two pieces of paper. On one I had coloured a big green circle and written the word 'YES' neatly below it. On the other, I had coloured a big red circle and written the word 'NO'. These I placed on the table, with the words facing him.

'Ok, Chris. I told you I'm listening,' I started, wanting him to be able to focus on what I was going to try to explain. 'This is for no. I'm going to put it to this side of you.' I put the red circle just to his right side, so that he could easily see it.

'Now, this one is for yes and I'm going to put it to your other side.'

I had thought and thought about how Chris could 'talk' without kicking me. One, I was a little tired of getting bruised. But also, sometimes he couldn't control his kicks, so if he was using them to say no, it wasn't a good system. How could you know when he was telling you something, or just having a spasm?

He had the most control over his head and eyes, so if he could understand me, maybe he would be able to use his head to talk to me more easily. At least, I was crossing my fingers that it would work.

'Ok. There are so many things I want to ask you, and I just know there are lots of things you want to tell me, but we've got to test it out first. Look at the red side for no and the green side for yes.'

Chris was smiling and his limbs jerked as they always did when he seemed excited, or when something new happened.

'Is your name Chris?' I asked.

His answer was clear and immediate. His head hit the left side of his head rest several times.

'Is your name Philip?' I asked.

Chris's head hit the right side.

'I knew it!' Tears came to my eyes and I jumped up to hug him as well as I could around his prison of a chair.

My heart was breaking for all of the years he had not been able to say to anyone something as simple as yes or no. So many weeks I had spent pouring my life out to Chris, and not asking him a single thing. He had so patiently listened. I knew what it was like to want to talk, and not have anyone to talk to. At least I had the words to do it. What did Chris have hidden inside him, bursting to be said? I hugged him tight while my tears soaked his shoulder.

When I came away though, he was just smiling his familiar lopsided grin as if nothing was all that different.

I didn't have time to share my discovery with Mr Jenkins before I had to head off to P.E. I was still pretty shaky with excitement and sadness anyway and besides, as sure as I was that there had been a breakthrough with Chris, Mr Jenkins's reaction to my last revelation made me a little wary of rushing in to tell him more. I had to have solid evidence before I showed anyone our crude communication system.

Last period, I was seeing Dr Sharon again. Maybe I would say something to her. Apparently there was something called 'client confidentiality', which Dr Sharon had explained meant that anything I said to her could not be shared with anyone else.

It was getting easier to talk to her now. She had this way of not even asking me anything, and yet somehow I ended up talking about things I hadn't even meant to talk about.

Today was like that. I walked in having decided to confide in Dr Sharon about my lunch hour with Chris – and I did start to talk about just that. I told her in detail about how I had planned the test, thinking about how Chris would be able to communicate with me if he was able to comprehend words.

'It was amazing. He can actually understand me!'

Dr Sharon was sitting forward in her seat; still and fully listening as usual. She never reacted with more than subtle facial expressions to anything I said, and it was the same now. She smiled slightly but didn't offer any comment. I sometimes wondered if I revealed I was an axe murderer in these sessions if she would just nod and encourage me to go on speaking.

'Just think of what Chris can say if he has a way to say it! I just *know* I'm going to be able to make his life so much better.'

'It feels good to help other people,' Dr Sharon commented.

'And that's what I'm going to do at home too. My mom is never going to have to go back into the hospital again.'

I had not meant to say this at all. It just fell out.

I really did feel more hopeful this time. Mom seemed so much calmer than usual. She hadn't once been sarcastic or snappy with Grandma like she usually was. And she wasn't staying up late pacing around. She had even done a little housework on Sunday, almost like a normal mom.

It had made me want to work especially hard to make sure that I kept her calm and well.

'I'm going to totally listen to her, so I can know right away if something is bothering her. She can get so frantic about things if they aren't fixed immediately.'

'What things would bother her, Jo?'

'Anything really. It could be that the kettle isn't working.' I thought back to the time that had happened. It had sparked her to check all of the appliances, finding that the iron, which we hadn't used in ages, also didn't work. And that had led to a two-day rant on how multinational companies were keeping everyone slaves to consumerism.

'Small things can kind of tip her over the edge. But if I'm there to know the small things that bug her, she will be better. And I know her; I know the things that have to be right to keep her well.'

'Like making sure the kettle is working,' Dr Sharon stated.

'Yep.'

'And what if it isn't working? What would you do?'

'I'd hide it and make her tea in the microwave. And then I'd buy a new one before she noticed it was gone.'

'Do you notice something?' she hinted. 'Your relationship with your mom and the one you are creating with Chris are pretty similar aren't they?'

'What do you mean?' My defences rose up.

'You want to fix them both.'

'That's not true!' I denied. 'Is it a crime to hope someone's life can be better?'

'Sometimes you need to take the kettle to the repair shop because you are not a small appliance mechanic.'

'What does that mean?' I felt annoyed. Dr Sharon usually just nodded in agreement when I spoke. Why was she trying to make me feel bad, just when everything in my life was going so well?

'Jo, it sounds like you are a fantastic help to your mom and to your friend. But Chris is Chris, and your mom is your mom. Not everything can be fixed.'

I didn't respond. She was getting everything wrong.

'Ok. We'll leave that,' she said. 'What about you? Who is in your life helping you?'

'I'm fine. I don't need any help.'

I realised that the people I had thought were helping me – Mr Jenkins, Dr Sharon – were as useless as anyone else who had ever tried to help me. They didn't understand me, and I didn't need them.

The only thing is, as I left Dr Sharon that day I had this feeling in the centre of my stomach that wasn't there when

I went in to see her. It was the feeling that I might not be in as much control of my world as I wished I was.

CHAPTER FOURTEEN

Each day with Chris there was new excitement. I would help him eat as quickly as he could manage, gulping down my own food in between Chris's mouthfuls, so that we could work on learning to talk to each other. Using the red and green dot system, I had asked him question after question about things that I definitely knew the answers to. I had wanted to be sure that Chris was getting it.

He was. His eyes were focused when we worked on questions, just like when he was painting.

After a couple of days of questions like, *Am I sitting on a chair?,* though, he stopped answering me. His eyes were no longer on me and he wouldn't move his head to either side.

I was quicker to figure him out now though. He was bored. What was the point in answering questions like these? It was probably more interesting for him when I rattled on and on about my life and didn't ask him a thing.

So I started to ask Chris about things I wanted to know.

'Do you have any brothers or sisters?'

No, he didn't.

'I don't either. It's just me and my mom.' I was so used to

being the odd one out with no siblings; it was nice to find out I wasn't so alone.

'Does your dad live with you?'

No. Another way we were the same! I didn't go as far as asking whether he *had* a father. As open as Mom was with me, this was one area she refused to answer any questions about.

'So is it just you and your mom?'

No.

I was a bit stumped by this one and thought maybe I had read an answer wrong, or that Chris had made a mistake in answering, so I went on to other questions.

'Ok. A bit about me. I'm thirteen, for forever it seems. Fourteen in a couple of months though.' I had shared so much personal stuff, but this is the first time I'd told Chris any of the usual facts. 'How old are you? Oh, sorry, that won't work. Are you thirteen? Fourteen? Fifteen? Are you saying fifteen?'

I had to ask each age and wait for the answer. Chris was fifteen. I had been able to get to the answer, but it was terribly tedious if this was the only way to communicate. Plus, I had to ask all the questions. He couldn't ask me anything. There had to be a better way for us to talk.

I had lots of questions to ask Mr Jenkins about Chris now. I wanted to know so much more about him, but I also wanted to have more avenues for things to talk to Chris about. If I had a bit more information, I would at least have some clues as to things to ask.

'Mr Jenkins, who does Chris live with?' I interrupted him from his marking of the assignment I had handed him during our science class.

'He lives in a group home for kids with physical and intellectual disabilities.'

'Oh.' That explained the difficulty I had run into with my questions about his family. 'So does his mom live nearby? Does he see her often?'

'That's kind of confidential stuff, Jo. I can't ask Chris if it would be okay to talk to you about his family, or lack of family.' Maybe he couldn't ask him, but I could.

I had decided not to let Mr Jenkins in on our communication lessons. At first I had wanted enough evidence to prove him wrong about Chris's abilities to understand and be understood. Now though, I was feeling kind of protective of the fragile strand of connection that I shared with Chris. He had chosen to talk to me, and I didn't want to give up our secret. I was afraid that it might be taken out of my control before we could explore where it might lead.

'Is asking how he gets to school confidential?'

'I guess not. The home he lives in has a special van that lifts Chris's chair onto it. The staff who work at his home drop him off and pick him up every day in the van.'

'Like the way wheelchairs get on the bus?' I had been on

the bus when it came to a stop where someone in a wheelchair wanted to get on. The whole bus lowered down, the person wheeled on and then the bus lifted up again.

'Same kind of thing, only the lift is hydraulically raised and lowered, rather than the bus.'

'What does he do at home? Like, does he have anything he's interested in?' I launched into another question.

'Now you are getting outside of my knowledge. There's a dividing line between school and home, same as for you,' Mr Jenkins said. 'I could probably arrange for you to go and visit Chris in his home though if you are interested.'

'Cool. I'd like that.'

* * *

Things were better than they had ever been at home. I was making sure of that.

I still left the house before Mom began to stir, but I made sure that her medication was ready for her, and that her favourite breakfast, French toast and bacon, was prepared and ready to be put in the microwave when she woke up. Then I rang her after first period class.

'Wake up call, Mom,' I said, trying to sound as cheerful as possible.

'Thanks, Jo,' she mumbled, never much of a morning person.

'What are the plans for today?' Every night I helped her to

write down what she was going to do while I was at school. For once Mom was going along with something that might actually help her.

After talking with Dr Sharon I had thought about what it was that often began Mom's spiral into uncontrollable thoughts and feelings. She had too much time on her hands. A job was not a possibility. She always ended up quitting or being fired. Mom didn't value things that employers usually felt were important, like being on time and staying until quitting time.

She also wasn't even able to operate in the normal world of filling time with the things that needed to get done: cleaning the house, cooking, doing the shopping, paying the bills. These had been my concerns as long as I had been able to do those things. I supposed it must have been Grandma who made sure the major things were done before that. I remembered there used to be a cleaning lady who came in once a week, which Mom had hated, and eventually she had literally chased her out, with a broom.

So Mom needed a project. She needed something to focus her energy and mind.

She could spend days or weeks obsessively learning about something she was interested in, writing copious notes that filled every surface in the house. This could be dangerous territory though because she was usually interested in some controversial cause that got her all upset. And she usually got upset in a crazy sort of way.

Plus she needed to see people. When she was in the routine of going to the drop-in mental health clinic she was always more steady, but she usually only did this in spurts, when she was focused on being normal, mostly for my sake. And this could lead to rants about her guilt about being a crazy mother. So, going to the clinic was not ideal either.

Mom had come up with a project herself. She was developing a series of workshops for kids to introduce the classic children's books. Then she planned to go to the libraries and community centres to see about putting them on.

'It's *The Lion, the Witch and the Wardrobe* today, Jo,' Mom said, suddenly sounding much more awake. 'So many great characters. What do you think about getting some kiddies designing costumes of their favourite character?'

'Sounds great!'

It was good to hear her so excited about something kind of productive – and at 9.30 in the morning instead of 2a.m.

CHAPTER FIFTEEN

I was looking for an upgrade to Chris's language. We no longer needed the red and green dots, as we both had it down – left yes, right no, but it just wasn't good enough. And it left me almost completely in the lead as far as initiating conversation.

I'd tried to look things up on the library computers before school started, but I couldn't find anything in the fifteen minutes at a time that I had. Sometimes I wished Mom wasn't so dead set against having a computer. It wasn't just that it was another thing that made me weird, not having one, but also it was so much harder for me to find things out. She preferred more old-fashioned ways of getting information.

It was Saturday and Mom and I were browsing the bookshelves of the maze-like second hand bookshop downtown. Despite the technology gap in my life, this was something I truly did like doing with Mom – spending hours looking through old books. It was a nostalgic feeling. We had been coming here for years; it was quite likely this had been my first outing as a baby. I loved the smell when I opened a very old book, and I loved going along just reading the titles on the spines, guessing at what the story might be about. We could spend hours here. It's a good thing I liked books; I'd say Mom would have disowned me if I didn't.

I was on a mission today though. While Mom scoured the shelves for children's books, I was in the nonfiction section, looking for books that might teach me a different way to talk with Chris.

I started with language, thinking maybe there was some kind of sign language we could use. Lots of foreign language dictionaries. I supposed it was a foreign language Chris and I had to formulate, but speaking in French or Spanish was still going to be speaking. Finally, I found some books on typical sign language interspersed in the language section, but this was not going to be helpful either. Chris just didn't have enough control of his limbs to sign anything.

So I scanned the shelves until I got to a tiny label – Disability. There were only a handful of books here. *Down Syndrome Explained. Child Development. Special Education Handbook.* I scanned through this one, but it was all to do with challenging behaviour – whatever that was.

I picked up a bulky binder, not a book at all, labelled PECS. At first I was just confused. There were only a few pages of instructions at the front and the rest of the binder was filled with pages of squares showing stick-like pictures of things. I turned to the front page again. Pictorial Exchange Communication System.

* * *

On Monday, I pulled out the little stick pictures I had pains-takingly redrawn and cut into squares at the weekend. There were twelve of them to represent twelve words: painting, eating, drinking, finished, happy, sad, and then six colours.

The idea was that you put some of these little squares on a board or in a book and then if someone couldn't speak, they could point to pictures to let people know what they wanted or needed. I wasn't sure how this system would be any better for Chris. It would be difficult for him to point at a picture, even with his good arm. I could maybe put out two pictures and he could choose one of them – left or right, but what if I didn't have out the picture he wanted? I was a bit stuck as to what to do next, so I thought we might as well try it.

I wasn't prepared for how Chris would react.

As soon as I took out the pictures, he started to thrash his head forcefully to one side. It was so sudden and so intense I was sure it must be one of the seizures that Mr Jenkins had told me about. He had said that Chris would thrash about even more than usual.

But he had also said that Chris's eyes would roll back and that he would probably drool excessively or even have some foam at the corners of his mouth. He wasn't doing this. His arms and legs were moving a normal amount for when he was excited, but it was mostly his head that was moving rhythmically to one side.

To the right side. To the no side. I suddenly understood that Chris was telling me NO.

'Chris, Chris!' I tried to get him to pay attention to me and stop banging. 'I'm listening; you're saying no! But stop!'

He did stop.

'Okay, just to be sure. Do you want to use these pictures?'

No.

'Do you know these pictures?'

Yes.

'Do you hate these pictures?'

Yes.

So that was the end of that. Maybe we were going to be stuck with 'yes' and 'no' as our only way to talk. I did wish I knew why Chris was so vehement about not using the pictures. What had happened to make him hate them so much?

CHAPTER SIXTEEN

Mom had run into her first problem since coming home from the hospital. It was a problem that should have been easy to solve, but of course nothing was ever that easy with my mom. Her newest obsession in her series of children's book workshops was focused on *Little Women*. She was stuck on how she could get kids interested in it and wanted my help, but I had never read it.

'If you think it won't work, Mom, don't include it. You said eight books, eight workshops. Just pick another book,' I persuaded.

'This is THE most important book of the lot! Your name came from it, Jo. Strong women protagonists in an age where it wasn't expected. It's SO important that the workshop must be perfect. There mustn't be a child who leaves the day without loving this book,' she insisted, gesturing widely for emphasis.

I was getting worried. Mom didn't deal well with dilemmas that could not be solved quickly.

'Okay. I'll just have to read it and we'll come up with something amazing when I'm done.'

'You better be fast about it, Jo. You never know when I'll lose the inspiration to finish this.'

It was a threat. If I couldn't help her out of her dilemma, then our easy days together would be over. I read into the night, trying to finish it. It didn't help that it was the longest book of the bunch.

I had finally succumbed to sleep, and so the next day the book was not finished. I knew that I had to finish it before the end of the day, or there was a good chance that it would be a very bad evening with Mom.

I spent the day hiding the novel behind text books, trying to read it as quickly as I could. I had even had to try to sneak in reading with Chris during lunch, apologising and reading some out loud to him in consolation.

Now it was the last period of the day and I was supporting Chris in art. I was frantic to finish the book, so that I could spend the time on the bus ride home thinking up some brilliant plan to get kids interested in it.

'Sorry, Chris. I really am going to have to read this last chapter while I help you with painting,' I apologised again, propping the book open with a block of wood I had found. I put it just behind his paper, so that I would be able to help him load his paintbrush and guide his arm as needed, while still sneaking in a quick sentence or two in between.

I held Chris's arm over the paint palette, reading as I waited to feel the familiar pull or push of his arm, guiding me to the colour he wished to use. I was nearly two paragraphs in when I realised that his arm was still.

I looked up. Chris's eyes were on the book and his head was gently tapping, 'Yes.'

'The book?'

The yes got more emphatic.

'Do you want me to read to you?'

No. Quick and clear.

I mulled this over. I was getting better at not trying to guess what Chris meant to say; and to just keep asking questions. I was learning that he almost never made a mistake in answering me, and that he often had very specific things to say, which entailed me asking just the right questions. Sometimes it took awhile.

'Do you want to paint on the book?'

No, and a big grin.

I couldn't think what to ask. I looked back over to him. His eyes were moving slowly left to right, left to right, focused on the book. I watched him, fascinated. After several more left to right scans, his eyes stopped moving and he communicated *yes* with his head.

Almost afraid to breathe, I brought the book right up to Chris and turned the page. Again his eyes scanned the page. He wasn't interested in painting today. He wasn't even interested in me today. Chris was reading.

* * *

I couldn't believe it at first. How was it possible the teachers, who I supposed knew Chris pretty well, did not know that he could read? How was it possible that they thought he didn't even understand most of what they said?

I went back to testing him.

'Does this word say look?' No. The word in front of Chris was jump.

He put up with this for a few words, correctly identifying all of them, and then he stopped answering me. He was not interested in impressing me. Obviously he was not interested in impressing anyone, or he would have found a way to do just that, years ago.

So I brought him books instead. We didn't have much time during lunch if we waited until we were finished eating to start reading. So I held the book Chris had chosen up for him, while feeding him with the other hand. I ate my own lunch in bits as I walked down the hallways between classes.

Still, he would communicate *no* to me if I brought out the book before I told him about the previous evening with Mom.

'Last night was good, Chris. She has finally moved on from *Little Women*. *Charlotte's Web* is easy for her. Making webs with wool and writing words with sparkle glue. That sort of thing.'

'And my mom talked to my grandma. I think they may even be almost liking each other. Mom actually laughed.'

'Okay. That's it really. Want to read now?'

And Chris would tap *yes*. I had brought several choices the first day. As he had such definite ideas on things as specific as paint colour I had expected that he would have certain tastes in books. He didn't. He wanted to read everything.

But then, I suppose that made sense. He had probably never been able to read a complete book before. How many times had he only been able to read the few pages of a book that someone in his line of sight was reading?

How did you even learn how to read if everyone around you thought you weren't able to even understand what was said to you, let alone have the capacity to read?

Mr Jenkins helped to answer that question.

During one science lesson, the picture symbols I had made fell out of my science text. I tried to hide them away, but Mr Jenkins had seen them.

'I see you haven't given up on Chris yet,' he commented. 'You should have asked. We have a computer program, where you can print out as many of those as you want. Quite a few of the kids use PECS in all sorts of different ways.'

'You kind of said that Chris can't understand anyway,' I defended.

'I didn't say that, Jo,' he said. 'He tests low in intelligence all right, but how can someone respond to an IQ test with no words? Besides, it is very important that everyone has a way to communicate.'

'Well, why hasn't anyone taught him anything?' I retorted, slamming down my text, angry again that Chris seemed so misunderstood.

'There's a lot you don't know about Chris. He spent his whole primary school years in an integrated classroom. He was part of every reading lesson, every math lesson.'

'And?'

'He hasn't been without opportunity, Jo. He had a teacher who lobbied very hard to get him an electronic picture exchange device that he could operate with a head switch. Lots of resources went into training people to use it. Everyone else used it. Chris would not. Or, to give him the benefit of the doubt, maybe he could not.'

I could believe that. If there was one thing I was learning about Chris, it was that he could be stubborn when he wanted to be. And he was not about to do anything just to please someone else. Not unless it was his idea.

* * *

I was trying something new with Chris. I had got the idea when my phone started beeping the night before, making me jump. I was always surprised when my phone beeped; it wasn't like I had any friends to send me text messages. When I checked it, sure enough it was just my service provider letting me know of some new deal.

But it gave me a thought. Could we use the same idea that

the phone keyboard utilised, for Chris to 'write' messages?

So now I had eight cards in front of Chris, each with either three or four letters on them. Abc, def, ghi and jkl on one side, mno, pqrs, tuv and wxyz on the other, with a big black line between the two groups. Chris had his eyes down and had a decidedly negative expression on his face. I was not sure if this was because of the cards in front of him, or because I had put the book he was reading away.

'You have to trust me, Chris,' I lectured. 'I'm trying to come up with a way you can *really* talk to me. Do you think I want to keep rattling on, with never a word from you?'

Chris raised his eyebrows, but didn't smile.

'Can you just try it?'

It took a few seconds, but finally he tentatively tapped to the left – *yes*.

'Thanks, Chris. Okay, let's start with your name.' I wrote his name in black letters across a paper. 'Is the first letter on this side?' I asked, pointing to one side of the black line. I eliminated four cards and then separated the remaining four cards with the black line.

'This side?' With each answer, I eliminated half the cards. Then I had to go through each letter on the final card. And that was for the first letter of the word. I counted. Thirty questions in order to spell CHRIS. It was not the most efficient system. No text prediction.

'It's just a prototype. To see if letters work for you,' I

appeased. He was being unusually patient with yet another of my tests. 'Anything you want to say?'

He started to move his head to the right, and then gave two taps to the left – *yes*.

I carefully pointed to each group of cards until I was down to one and then asked about each letter on the remaining card, writing down the letter he indicated yes to, then bringing back all eight cards again to guess the next letter. D, O, N, E, N, O, W. It had taken nearly five minutes to communicate, 'Done now.'

Chris smiled and I started to giggle.

'Guess you won't be rambling on for ages like me with this system,' I conceded. 'We're going to have to find some twenty-first-century technology – and fast. Or it'll take you until dinner time to let someone know what you want for breakfast!'

At least Chris was developing a bit of a sense of humour about my crude attempts at helping him talk.

CHAPTER SEVENTEEN

I couldn't believe that it was only a month until Christmas. For once, I wasn't worrying about when everything would fall apart. Mom had been home since just before Halloween, without any major crises. And for the first time ever, I was not counting the days down to the school holidays. I was too busy trying to make Chris's home-made communication system work as best as I could, while finding out about computer programs and devices for people with physical disabilities. I had found a few things on the internet, hurrying into the library before school to do a quick search, but mostly searching for anything about nonverbal communication – that's what it was called – brought me back to the hated picture symbols.

Mr Jenkins's tiny office off the resource room was a goldmine of information though. As the head of the special education department, all of the flyers and catalogues and sales information were addressed to him. Most of the time he was not even in his office and the door was open so that he could fly in, grab whatever thing was needed from the growing pile on his desk, and fly out again.

I first discovered the gems of information dispersed throughout this pile of papers when Mr Jenkins sent me to fetch the marking book he had forgotten for science. I had to gently move quite a few papers and books before I found the purple-covered marking book where he kept track of assignment and test scores. While I was moving things, a glossy catalogue caught my attention because the boy on the cover was in a wheelchair very similar to the one Chris used. I tucked it under my arm along with the found marking book.

'Can I look at this?' I casually asked Mr Jenkins.

'Hundreds where that came from. You are welcome to keep them all,' he said. 'I'm drowning in advertisements, and truthfully, I don't want to look at things I only wish our budget would stretch to.'

I half listened, scanning the computer aid and device section. Bingo! There were three pages dedicated to different ways to control a mouse or to type on a computer *without your hands*. I couldn't believe my luck!

This is why I hadn't been able to find anything on the internet! I had been looking for some kind of fantastical system, when all I needed to look for was a simple way for Chris to use what everyone else used for communication – a computer.

My heart sank when I noticed the prices of the eye tracking and head tracking devices. There was nothing for under $1,000. And I remembered Mr Jenkins talking about all of the money that had gone into technology for Chris that he had refused to use. This coupled with what Mr Jenkins had just said about the budget. It wasn't sounding hopeful that Chris's communication needs would be met through school.

So Chris and I trudged along using our 'phone texting' model, tweaking it as we practised. We were now using it more like the phone set up, with Chris tapping between one and eight times to choose a group of letters, and then between one and four taps to choose a letter. It still was cumbersome. It was hard for him to be precise with his taps, and so sometimes I guessed wrong on the group of letters. Plus, the yes/no system still worked best for a lot of things, and I got confused as to whether Chris was indicating yes or no, or choosing a letter to spell something.

And then, he wasn't very good at spelling either. He may have learned the basics of reading and writing by observing all through primary school, but without any practice, he was pretty rusty. After a few days of using the new text system, I had carefully written out each letter Chris chose, ending up with 'Creeps'. I had spent ten minutes trying to ask the right yes/no question to find out who he was talking about. Finally he just stopped answering me.

It was only at home that night, as I started to prepare dinner for Mom and I that I realised what Chris had meant – crêpes. My savoury crêpes were one of his favourites, and he was requesting them for the next day.

And some days, Chris just didn't want to talk, and then he wouldn't. Nothing could budge him.

But mostly, he just got tired quickly. It seemed difficult for him to concentrate for very long. After nearly a month of practising, he still only spelled out single words or very short phrases for me. Yet, I knew from the pace at which he powered through novels, that his understanding was way beyond short phrases.

It was a beginning though, and whenever I could, I mined Mr Jenkins's office for new catalogues, hoping to find some devise with a price tag reasonable enough for me to suggest it to Mr Jenkins.

I had laid out the letter cards one day, when Mr Jenkins opened the door just enough to pop his head in, obviously on his way to somewhere else. I tried to sweep the cards under my binder, without drawing any attention to them.

'Hi, Mr Jenkins. I'll bring Chris's dishes and stuff to the kitchen at the end of lunch,' I blurted, trying to keep eye contact with him so he wouldn't focus on the table.

'Right?' he said suspiciously. 'You've pretty much done that since you started, but thanks for the info.'

I froze as his gaze travelled down to the table.

'Looks like I'm interrupting some sort of game here, so I won't keep you now. I just wanted to say that Chris's house staff finally got back to me, and you can go for a visit to his house any time this week. Just name the day.'

'Tomorrow,' I answered immediately.

'Righty-oh.' He went to leave and then poked his head back in. 'Oh, and any time you want to let me in on the game, Jo, just let me know, okay?'

* * *

That night I arrived home with an idea to make sure Mom would be out of the house the whole next day, thinking about something else, before I broached the subject of doing something after school. It made my stomach do back flips just thinking about the last time I had dared not come straight home. I had even stopped going to my cabin since Mom had come home. I couldn't leave her for too long. So on the bus I had gone over how I would say my idea, hoping that she would go for it. If not, I was not going to be able to visit Chris. I just couldn't risk putting Mom over the edge again, no matter how good her mental health might seem.

I waited until dinner was done and Mom had her notepad and the last of her chosen eight children's books, sprouting sticky-note feathers in every direction, in front of her. I sat down and took the pile of workshop plans she had finished – well, as finished as they were ever going to be. She kept going back to them and adding ideas for projects and plays and songs. As the rate she was going each workshop was going to end up being a year-long course.

'Mom, I think these are great.' I did mean it. The ideas

she had thought up would make any kid interested in books. 'Don't you think it's time to see where you could advertise the workshops? We could make a list of all the places that could be interested.'

'Oh, I don't know, Jo,' Mom answered, her head almost touching her current book of interest as she carefully turned pages, pink highlighter in hand. 'Do you think there's enough here yet to compete with computers and video games?'

'I do. And I'd say community centres and libraries will be putting together their calendars for January now.'

I had no idea if this was true. I hoped it was, or at least that people at enough of them would talk to Mom long enough to keep her out of the house all afternoon.

'Yeah?'

I had made enough of a point to entice her to look up from her book.

'What about making a list tonight and going around to places tomorrow? You only have to show them a sample idea, a workshop you're most happy with.'

'I suppose it couldn't hurt.'

'How about I meet you down town at six for a celebration dinner out? Grandma gave me a little money for a rainy day. We can use it for a sunny day instead!'

I hadn't even had to mention my visit to Chris.

CHAPTER EIGHTEEN

I was waiting outside the school for Chris when the white van pulled up. A shortish, stoutish woman, who looked about fifty, got out, opened the back doors and used a control to lower a metal ramp. I assumed this must be Chris's way home.

Flo wheeled a grinning Chris out, handing the woman his backpack.

'A good day,' Florence said. 'We need some more protective gloves when you get a chance; we're almost out.'

'Okay. I'll let Mary know,' the woman replied. 'No seizure yet, huh?'

'Nope. It's been a couple of weeks hasn't it? We're in for a big one I'd say.'

Neither woman seemed to notice that I was there, or that they seemed to be talking about Chris even though he was right there.

But Florence *had* noticed me standing a few paces away because she gestured me over, and introduced me to the van driver.

'Cynthia, this is Jo, our newest unpaid member of staff,

wanting to see what goes on in the residential side of things.'

That wasn't what I was wanting at all. I just wanted to know more about *Chris*. It wasn't like I was doing this for some sort of work experience.

'Hi, Jo,' the woman said, holding out her hand to shake mine. 'You're most welcome. We've been hearing that Chris has quite taken to you.'

'We get on okay,' I said, looking over at Chris, who didn't seem to be paying attention to anything we were saying.

It felt weird to be talking with Florence and Cynthia, as if Chris were not even there. It was like talking behind someone's back, only the person was right in front of you and you just couldn't see them. It was as if they just couldn't see Chris.

Cynthia didn't talk much in the van. Instead, she turned up the radio, tuned into classic rock, and sang along to the songs she knew. I was glad for that.

We stopped one more time, to pick up a younger girl from an elementary school. She was in a wheelchair as well. Hers was pink and tiny. She was tiny too. I thought she couldn't be more than six or seven, with delicate little features and skin so pale it seemed almost translucent.

'This is Lucy,' Cynthia introduced when we were all back in the van.

'Hi, Lucy,' I greeted her, but there was no response from her whatsoever.

Cynthia and I sat in the only two seats at the front of the van. The whole back of the van was open, with metal strips running from back to front where straps could be fitted in slots, attached to parts of the wheelchairs, and ratcheted tight so the chairs didn't move or tip over while we were driving.

We drove on for another ten minutes or so, Cynthia singing or humming the whole way, and then turned into the drive at a big bungalow. Mr Jenkins had given me directions from this house to the nearest bus stop, so I more or less knew where it was in town. I hadn't known what to expect though; maybe something more hospital-like? This just looked like an ordinary house, with a bit of a flower garden and yellow curtains in every window. The drive was big and there were three cars parked outside, but then, the house looked pretty big too, big enough that it could be a home for a very large family.

When I followed Cynthia and Lucy in, pushing Chris's chair, I immediately knew that this was not an ordinary family home. It was more a feeling than anything that I could see. Things just didn't seem quite right to be a usual home. The walls were painted a warm lilac colour, which coordinated with the yellow and lilac curtains, and yet the tile floor seemed too institutional for the soft colours above it. Plus, there didn't seem to be any of the knick-knacks that would usually be in such a coordinated house. No paintings, no shelves or china cabinets with ornaments, no photos on the wall. It was just – pretty but empty.

Part of what contributed to the empty feeling was how big and open the room that we had entered was. It was huge. There was a table that would fit more than eight people on one side of the room, with what looked like a normal-sized kitchen in an L shape at the end. On the side we had just entered there was a very small sofa and a large television. That was the only furniture in the room. But when I looked around I could see why it needed to be so big and so open. Besides Lucy and Chris, there were three other kids in wheelchairs in the room. I had never seen so many wheelchairs in one place before – not even in the SE. They took up a lot of space.

There was another woman in the kitchen and she came out when we arrived.

'Hi, Lucy, Hi, Chris,' she greeted, with actual eye contact and a bit of a squeeze to each arm. 'Hi, Jo. I'm glad you could come!'

For the first time since leaving the school, I felt that I might be welcome here. And I was relieved to see that someone in Chris's house actually talked directly to him. This woman was very young; she didn't look much older than me. She was dressed in jeans and a hoodie that I wished I had myself.

'Sit down,' this woman invited. 'I'm Alison, and, before you sit down actually, come meet Chris's housemates.'

I was introduced to Jamie, Teresa and Sam. Most were not

able to talk, or at least they didn't greet me, but Alison made eye contact with each one as she introduced them and gave a small bit of information to me, almost as if they were introducing themselves.

'Jamie is the oldest here. He's actually leaving us for better things soon, aren't you, Jamie?' Alison said, smiling at him. He gave the slightest grin back.

'And this is Teresa.' Alison had led me over to a girl, whose wheelchair had a kind of a tray over it, with symbols similar to the ones I had tried to use with Chris on it. 'Want to say hi Teresa?'

Teresa's hand hovered over the tray for a few seconds, and then hit one of the buttons. It lit up and an electronic voice said,

'Hi. I am Teresa. I am very happy to say hello.'

I was intrigued by this and wanted to ask more questions, but Alison moved me along to meet the last housemate, who was stationed in front of the television, watching cartoons.

'And this is Sam, who was our baby until Lucy joined us a month ago. He's a little jealous, aren't you Sam?' she teased.

I was surprised to hear him respond, beginning to assume that all of Chris's housemates were nonverbal.

'Am not Aly!' he denied, 'I'm ten and she's only six you know.'

'I know, Sam-my-man. Just teasing. A game of basketball after supper?'

'I'll win, you know,' Sam informed me.

'Yep. It's in my job description: lose to Sam in basketball every shift.'

Sam chuckled.

When I looked around, Chris had disappeared. I assumed that he must be with Cynthia, since she had also disappeared. So I decided to sit down at the table as Alison had invited. It was kind of weird that someone would just disappear without telling you. Of course Chris couldn't tell me, but shouldn't someone else have told me for him?

Alison had headed back into the kitchen, obviously making dinner. There were three kids parked in various spots in the big room, and only one – Sam, who seemed to be doing anything, even if it was only watching television. I wanted to bring them all around the table, if only to make it seem that we were all having a cup of tea and a chat, not unlike what Grandma and I did when we were together – pretend we were talking.

I didn't though. There seemed to be definite, unspoken structure to this house. So I just sat for a few minutes, waiting to be told what was happening next. Then I got curious, and my curiosity overcame my apprehension. I headed down one of the two wide hallways leading from the main room, looking for Chris.

I found him all right. The first door off the hall was a bathroom with a wide door leading into it, and the door was open. There was Cynthia and another woman lifting Chris, whose jeans were down to his knees, onto a kind of a seat over the toilet. He didn't see me, but I certainly saw a lot more of him than I had been planning to.

I quickly stepped out of eyeshot, but not before one of the women helping Chris saw me.

'Be out in a minute,' she called casually, as if it were an everyday occurrence for visitors to see the occupants of the house with their pants down.

'Looking for a toilet.' I stumbled on the words of my excuse.

'Yep,' the same voice replied. 'Down the other hallway is the staff toilet.'

I didn't want to argue that I wasn't staff, just someone trying to have a normal visit with a friend. I hid in the staff bathroom for a few minutes, completely embarrassed. I couldn't stay there forever. Besides, even though I felt mortified, it had seemed that nobody else thought I had done anything wrong. So I took up my seat at the table again.

Eventually, Chris emerged, with the third woman pushing his chair. She parked him beside me, without even saying hi, and then wheeled Lucy away. I just nodded at Chris, not able to talk to him after the bathroom incident.

Cynthia appeared again, with a tray of small plastic cups filled with pills. She went to the kitchen, where Alison handed her a small dish of yogurt and came back to give

Chris the tablets from one cup, each of the five pills in a spoonful of yogurt. She then went to Sam and to Teresa, feeding them medication as well. Now this was normal life to me. Despite still feeling uncomfortable, I almost smiled to think that mine was not the only household dominated by medications.

'Do you want to help me in here, Jo?' Alison called from the kitchen.

I was glad to have something to do other than sit with Chris and wait for whatever was coming next, which probably involved taking care of some kind of physical need which I didn't need to know about. Alison had plates and bowls all over the counter. She was spooning some of the chicken that she had taken out of the oven into a blender.

'Can you put some potatoes on those seven plates please? You're eating with us, right?' she asked.

'Yeah, sure.'

I helped dish up the food, while Alison blended some of everything into mush and spooned it into two bowls.

Then it was a whirlwind of activity, with five wheelchairs being moved to the table, plates going on the table, assistants tying bibs. Three kids had to be fed, with only Sam and Teresa able to feed themselves, using special bowls that stuck on the table and adapted spoons to make it easier to get food from the bowl to their mouths. Every able-bodied person, including me, assuming my usual role of assisting Chris, had jobs to do. Dinner here was very different from our private lunch periods.

Still, with all of the feeding, wiping mouths and moving dishes so they didn't get overturned, the women working managed to keep up a steady stream of conversation, none of it relating to any of the kids and teens around the table.

'So what were you saying about her dress?' the woman who had not been introduced to me asked Cynthia.

'Oh, yeah,' she said, obviously picking up from an earlier conversation. 'She tried it on last night, after it came back more than a week later than the alterations were supposed to take, and you wouldn't believe it, Mary – it still isn't right!'

'No!' exclaimed Mary. 'Watch your milk now, Teresa!' I caught the plastic cup just before it toppled from the table.

Alison turned to me to explain what the conversation was about.

'Cynthia's daughter is getting married this weekend.'

'Mary! Mary! Mary!' Sam interrupted, waving his spoon toward her. Cynthia took his spoon, putting her finger to her mouth to indicate for Sam to shush.

'What's she going to do?' Mary asked, ignoring Sam and feeding Lucy another spoonful of mush.

'No choice. It just has to go back again and hope it's right by Saturday.'

The conversation continued like this, while everyone was fed at breakneck speed. With all of the activity going on,

Chris was thrashing non-stop. It was hard for me to dodge his limbs. I had learned by now that when he couldn't stop his arms and legs, I would just get as quiet as possible myself, relaxing every part of me and shutting up, and his body would start to slow down too. But it just wasn't working in this busy place. I wondered if it was always so chaotic.

After dinner, everything was the same, only in reverse. I wondered what the rush was. After all, it was only 4:30 and there was a whole evening yet!

I offered to help with dishes and clean-up, as Alison was in the kitchen again, and I thought she might be the best one to ask about what Chris did at home. Since Mary had emerged from a side room with a huge armload of laundry and started to fold it, and Cynthia was busy writing in a binder, Chris and most of his housemates were still parked around the table. Only Sam had been moved. He was in front of the TV again. I moved Chris's chair to the entrance to the narrow kitchen. His chair would not actually fit in the kitchen, but at least he was close enough to talk to as Alison and I worked at cleaning up the mound of dishes and mess.

'So what is Chris interested in? I know he likes painting, but what else?' I asked Alison, looking at Chris and adding, 'Is that okay to ask, Chris?'

He didn't smile or give any response to me. He wasn't looking at me. He didn't seem to be listening. Ever since we had left school it had been as if he had been unplugged. I couldn't read his facial expressions; it was as if he wasn't here with me at all.

'I'm pretty new here, and I only work when someone can't work,' Alison said, her brows coming together in concentration. 'Hmm. In the summer we went to a couple of music festivals and he seemed to like that? And he loves the bathtub, but only if it's super warm. He hates it when it gets cold! Right, Chris?'

I hardly had to know how warm he liked his bath water. It wasn't the usual information one needed to know about a friend.

'How about his family? Do they come and visit him?' I tried, stealing a look at Chris to see if he was listening. He seemed as tuned out as ever.

'Chris is a ward of the state,' said Alison. 'I can't remember exactly why. It's in his file. He's lived here for a few years though.'

I thought about that. Things might not be easy living with my mom, but at least I had one. Chris had no one. Alison seemed to be the nicest of the staff working here, and she didn't even seem to know him that well.

When everything was cleaned up, Alison wheeled Chris over to the television where Sam was.

'I'll be back,' she said to Chris. 'It's time for Jamie to get out of his chair.'

The staff never seemed to stop, and yet the kids here

145

seemed to be perpetually just waiting to be handled. I sat with Chris and Sam for twenty minutes, watching the cartoon that was on, while Alison, Mary and Cynthia came in and out of rooms, wheeling Teresa away next, then bringing her back, then wheeling Lucy away again.

Finally Cynthia came to take Chris away again.

'Chris is going to have a bath now,' Cynthia informed me. Informed *me*, didn't ask Chris if that was what he wanted to do. 'Do you want to help with that?'

I must have looked horrorstruck. I *felt* horrorstruck. I couldn't believe that she was actually asking me that. I was glad that Chris still seemed to be in a world of his own.

'I think I have to go now,' I managed to say.

I had seen enough. I had been sceptical about the prospects of anyone at school being able to get Chris the technology he needed to communicate, but I doubted that the staff here would have time to listen even if he had a way to talk. Here he was a body to be fed, toileted, bathed and medicated. How was being able to talk going to change that? I could suddenly understand why Chris had given up trying long ago.

CHAPTER NINETEEN

All I could talk about with Dr Sharon was Chris.

'It's terrible. I thought I lived in a prison, but Chris can't even decide when or where to *move* in his home.'

'You feel you live in a prison, Jo?'

'No, I'm talking about Chris!' Dr Sharon was annoying me again, trying to put words in my mouth, and not listening.

'So things are fine now at home,' she stated.

I felt my stomach lurch. I didn't want to think about home. Things *were* fine weren't they? Never mind that Mom had not spoken a word about her day of sales pitches to libraries and community centres. Maybe she was waiting for people to get back to her. Maybe she wanted to surprise me with her name printed in a calendar of upcoming classes: *Books Come Alive: A series of interactive workshops for children 5-12 where we will explore the classic stories of our time in exciting new ways. Suzanne MacNamara facilitating. Sue has a Masters Degree in English Literature and a lifelong love of books.* Maybe.

'Mom was a bit quiet over the weekend. But she's been working hard on her project, so I guess she needs a rest, right?'

Was I trying to convince myself? Mom had not gotten out of bed on Saturday until four. At twelve, after agonising over whether to wake her up or leave her sleeping, I had opted for letting her sleep. It meant she wasn't taking her medication on time, but I was afraid that if I woke her up to a bad day, then the day would have to be spent coaxing her out of whatever mood she was in. That could be unpredictable.

There was hardly any food in the house and I had started to worry about what to do if she didn't get up the next day either. In the end I thought it was safer to leave her sleeping, while I went for the groceries a day earlier than usual.

So I had gone to the supermarket, buying as much as I could carry in my backpack and two bags. The whole time I checked my watch and worried that Mom might be up and getting herself into a frantic mood that I might have been able to avert if I had been home. Then I worried that she might *not* be up yet, and it was getting later and later for her medication, and would that lead to more trouble that night?

The whole weekend had been like that. When Mom was awake, there were no big dramas, so that was good. It was only that she was *so* quiet, which had made me nervous, waiting for the storm after the calm.

In my heart I knew that something had not gone well Friday afternoon. We had met at the bookstore after I had left the group home, and we had gone off to Mom's favourite little Italian restaurant for dinner. Nothing that day had seemed terribly wrong – except that she had not mentioned a single word about her afternoon. But then, I had not asked her a single thing either. I had been too caught up in my own thoughts about Chris and where he lived.

I hadn't been able to stop seeing the image of him being lifted onto the toilet, without even the dignity of a closed door. What point was there in Chris being able to say a damn thing in that house? And that made me doubt the people who were in his life at school. Didn't Mr Jenkins keep telling me not to get my hopes up?

'Something *has* to change for Chris.' I emphatically changed the subject with Dr Sharon again. 'I can't stand to think of him living with no one understanding, no one even caring! Having to just survive until he gets to school!'

'Is it Chris we are talking about, or you, Jo?' She infuriated me! Why would she not listen to what I was saying?

'It all could fall apart and you don't even care!'

I jumped up and ran out. I couldn't stay any longer. I felt I was going to explode if I did.

* * *

The house was quiet when I walked in.

'Mom?' I called out. 'Are you home?'

There was no answer, but the light in the kitchen was on and Mom never left the lights on when she went out, so as to save fossil fuels. Funny how she could remember details like that all of the time, yet not be bothered to remember things like paying bills. I had picked up the phone bill from the mailbox and opened it on my way in. It was an overdue notice. Mom hadn't paid the bill, even though, when it had arrived two weeks ago she had assured me that she would pay it that very day. I had actually believed her.

I walked into the living room. The room was covered in torn up pieces of paper. Mom was sitting in the middle of the mess. Beside her was a red binder, yawning open and empty. I knew what it meant. That binder had been a familiar sight on our kitchen table over the last month. It used to hold all of Mom's notes, ideas and planned activities for her series of workshops. Now everything covered the living room floor instead.

She looked up. I expected that she would be sad, but no, I should have known. She was smiling.

'Well, that's finished! On to other things.'

'Why?' I asked tersely. I couldn't believe I had bothered being worried about her.

'Oh, Jo. You are so naïve.' She gave me that same smile. 'No one cares about books anymore.'

'So, no one was interested in the workshops?' I snapped this too. I was not in the mood for this after the session with Dr Sharon. All of the hours spent patiently helping Mom come up with ideas, praising her, urging her on, lay in ruins on the floor.

'I suppose not,' she said, casually flicking a torn piece of paper off her arm. 'I didn't actually get past a secretary or a desk clerk.'

'Because?'

'How should I know?' she shrugged. 'There was talk about forms and making appointments. You know I can't bear bureaucracy.'

'And so you just threw it all away, like you always do,' I stated. I went to walk away, to head toward my cabin. But instead of feeling the usual panic and confusion gripping my stomach, I felt red, hot anger. Clenching my fists, I spun around to face her again.

'Did it ever occur to you that people were rejecting you and not the workshop idea?' I wanted her to feel as hurt and humiliated as I had felt over and over again through the years living with her. I had always forgiven her; always put her first above anything in my life. I had thrown away any possibility of ever having a friend, so that she would be okay. For what?

'You are weird and selfish! You never care about anyone other than yourself! Why would anyone want to listen to you?!' I was screaming.

Mom was holding her head now, and rocking back and forth. She looked at me with imploring eyes. For once in my life, I didn't care. I didn't care if she ended up in the hospital tonight, even if it was my fault.

'Stop it, Mom! Or don't. You know, I don't care. Do what

you want, you always do!'

I stormed out. I was getting good at this walking out thing.

There wasn't any need to count now to get myself to my cabin. My anger focused me, and I wanted to get as far away from Mom as possible. I had tried so hard this time to make sure she was okay. But she wasn't willing to try herself.

Maybe Dr Sharon was right. My life was as dismal as Chris's was. But the difference was I could do something about it. I could do something about it for both me and Chris.

I didn't know how I would do it, but I would not let Chris stay in a house where no one cared about him. And I wasn't sure I wanted to stay in my own house any more. Mom didn't seem to care about anyone but herself. Somehow – I didn't know how yet – I was going to find a way to get Chris out of that awful house, even if it meant staying somewhere with him myself.

I stayed at the cabin until it was deep dark and I had to use the flashlight I kept there 'just in case', to make my way back down the river bank and the path to home. When I got back it was late, and all of the lights were off. The rage that had driven me out of the house had abated, but I still didn't want to see Mom, so I was glad that she seemed to be asleep.

I put my hand on the handle of her bedroom door, almost turning it to check that she was safe. It was hard to stop being Mom's carer. A glimmer of doubt about my plan threatened to grip me, but then the anger I had felt earlier bubbled up, and I dropped the door handle and went to bed myself instead.

CHAPTER TWENTY

I didn't sleep well. I woke up in the middle of the night with stomach pains and the apprehension of having no real plan of where Chris and I could go. It seemed like hours that I was awake, not opening my eyes, but thinking and thinking about where an almost fourteen-year-old girl could take a friend who is totally physically dependent on others and needs a way to be able to talk.

I must have drifted off to sleep at times though, because I had strangely real dreams of being in an alien ship with Chris. The aliens were trying to talk to us, to reassure us that everything was okay even though we were leaving earth. But we couldn't understand anything the aliens said. In the dream, Chris could talk and he kept yelling at them to speak his language. I was telling Chris to be quiet because I wanted to concentrate on understanding the aliens, but I was getting confused with all of his yelling.

When I finally opened my eyes to the light of morning, I had only a few minutes to hurriedly throw on some clothes and get out of the door to catch the school bus. If it wasn't that I didn't want to see Mom at all, I would have been tempted to go back to sleep.

Chris and I had art second period. I went to the art cupboard to get his supplies. We had moved on from the cheap children's paper to work on proper stretched canvas. I had not asked; I had simply opened cupboards until I found what I wanted, what other kids were using. I had flipped through the art books on one of the shelves, finding and tabbing all of the famous abstract paintings I could find, and had helped Chris to look at them. Some of them, he had spent ages looking at, his eyes moving over each detail.

Between the art appreciation exposure and some better materials, the results were surprising. Chris was experimenting with texture and colour and lines. He was developing a distinct style and he now would work on one canvas for several classes before indicating that he was done with it. Even the teacher had stopped completely ignoring us. He had taken to spending some time each class watching how Chris painted, as if he were trying to catch him out substituting someone else's work for his. During one class the week before he had actually suggested, to Chris, as if I were not there, that he might want to look at Miro's work to get some inspiration.

I tried my best to find our usual rhythm, feeling where Chris needed my help to guide his arm where he wanted it to go. To facilitate his painting, I had to stop thinking of anything but his painting arm. Usually it was so freeing to do that, but today that blank mind space was impossible to achieve. My mind kept skipping to where on the planet I could take Chris.

He looked up at me with a frown.

'I'm sorry, Chris,' I sighed. 'I'm just trying to think of how to help you.'

I didn't want to say more, now that the art teacher had taken more of an interest in Chris and might overhear. And what more could I say, when I didn't have a clue how I was going to help him, besides getting him out of a home that seemed to be breaking his heart? Just seeing him with such a downbeat expression made me want to wheel him out right then, forget about a plan. We could just start walking and not stop.

* * *

I didn't exactly miraculously come across a perfect solution to Chris's dilemma. Instead, I wrestled a glimpse of an idea out of the only education I had – the piles of brochures and catalogues and magazines that I had gleaned from Mr Jenkins's office over the weeks.

I had been staying in my room the last two days, avoiding Mom, who had become very quiet again. I had already gone to the cabin that afternoon, hoping that some brilliant idea would come to me, and I would know exactly how to help Chris. I had thought about just running away with him. But that was just ridiculous. He already had the disadvantage of not being able to walk or talk, but in his giant blue chair he was completely conspicuous as well. It wasn't like I could easily disappear with him.

So I was thinking and flipping through magazines and catalogues that I had brought home from Mr Jenkins's office. I wasn't even sure what I was looking for.

My whole dresser was covered in glossy papers now. I usually only had a moment between classes to collect any new papers that were strewn on Mr Jenkins's desk, so I tended to just grab everything. They ended up here at the end of each day.

Most of the brochures were completely irrelevant, advertising something like playground equipment, or preschool furniture. The catalogues often had a section on communication devices or adaptive technology – which meant things to help people say something when talking was difficult for them, and stuff to help people do things and use things when parts of their body didn't work. I was learning the lingo – both from the magazines and from just being in the SE wing. There was a whole language attached to kids with disabilities.

Within these sections, I tended to find the same things advertised. I knew what Chris needed, and it wasn't that complicated actually. He just needed a system that would let him type and move a cursor with his eyes. And it existed!

Then he just needed one of those programs that spoke typed words out. Oh – and in an ideal world, a word processing program with text prediction because of his terrible spelling and so it wouldn't take Chris so long to talk. All of this added up to lots of money though. More than I had. More than it sounded like it was possible to get from school.

But now I was looking for something different, so I was looking through the disability and education magazines – in desperation. Chris had bigger problems than just communication.

In the last few days, he just wasn't smiling like he usually did. He spent a lot of time frowning at me, and he wanted me to talk to him, instead of reading or communicating anything to me.

I had to find a place to take him to. And I didn't have a clue what options there might be out there.

It was an advert that caught my attention. Near the back of one of the magazines was a half page ad for a conference that only caught my eye because of the title, 'The Role of Communication Technology in Special Education: Reaching the Non-Verbal Child'. Then I noticed the date – this weekend. And then I noticed the venue – The Harrison Hotel, Hampton. That was only two hours away, and I realised excitedly that we could take the train! I could get Chris onto a train.

Reading the fine print, the conference was probably for teachers and people like that. I was sure it wasn't for kids looking for a new home. It wasn't a solution, but it was a direction. There was a blurb near the bottom saying *booths still available for representatives of special schools across the region*, so maybe there was a possibility of finding Chris something better? Surely at a conference about communication there would be someone, anyone, interested in helping Chris! I just needed to get him there, and I only had two days to figure out the details of how.

CHAPTER TWENTY-ONE

I woke up the next morning with a feeling of unease. I hadn't slept well again. Every thought, when I had woken in the night, had been to do with details of taking Chris away. But awake, in the real world, I was losing my nerve.

I would have thought I had inherited more of Mom's spirit of following her heart, doing what she thought was right for the moment, with no thought as to the practicalities. But mostly, much as I usually didn't like to admit it, a whole lot of the way I tackled each day was like Grandma, each decision weighed and analysed, always planning for the difficulties that probably would come up.

I got dressed slowly, at the same time reading the advert for the conference yet again. Was it completely crazy to think about taking Chris to it?

I still had the magazine in my hand when the door to my room burst open. I jumped, not expecting Mom to be awake at this hour of the morning.

'I thought that today would be the perfect day for you to stay home from school!'

I just looked at her in disbelief.

'Well don't look so excited!' she teased. 'When was the last time you had a proper day off? We could do something fun, something you would like to do.'

'I'd like to go to school,' I sighed.

'I don't know why you are suddenly so keen on going to school,' Mom sniffed, going on casually, 'We used to have that in common you and I – misfits in the old secondary school department. I looked forward to sharing school horror stories when you reached about twenty – old enough to realise the ridiculousness of the conformist agenda of it all.'

'How long have you known how unhappy I was at school?' This was news to me. I never told her anything about school.

'Well of course you would be forlorn, my awkward wildebeest in the midst of lions! It will make you far more interesting as an adult though.'

It had always been easy for me to not talk about school. Mom had hardly ever referred to my school life at all. She had certainly never asked about how happy I was. I had always assumed that she was too wrapped up in her own problems to even notice much about her daughter's life. From the time I was five I had instinctively tried to shield her from knowing how hard it was to face each school day. It had never occurred to me that she knew how miserable I was, and was actually *glad* about that.

'What's this?' she asked, picking up one of the brochures

strewn on my dresser.

'Do you really care?' I asked, snatching it out of her hands.

'Well, I suppose not, Jo.' She dropped the brochure on the floor. 'To be honest, you *have* been a bit boring lately. If it's because of this sort of thing, I suppose I don't really care.'

The words hit me in the stomach like a medicine ball shot out of a cannon. I had spent my whole life tuned into the slightest whim Mom might have. I had tried to sense any crack in her happiness before she even knew it herself, so that I might make sure that she didn't have to spend one minute unhappy if I could help it.

Now the one time that I cared about something, something important, she dismissed it without even wanting to know about it. Dealing with her difficulties coping with life was one thing, coping with complete rejection of who I was finding out I was, was quite another thing.

For once, I could not keep my composure with her. Blink as I might, I could not stop the tears that threatened to collapse me. She just looked at me, smiling a slow smile and raising her eyebrows.

'Oh, Jo, you must learn to control your emotions!'

* * *

I couldn't concentrate in science class with Mr Jenkins. Mom's words kept going through my head, and each time I said them to myself I became more determined to help

Chris. '*You must learn to control your emotions.*' Fear? Just control it. Worry about how Mom might be? Just control that.

It was the usual routine of me working on an assignment, while Mr Jenkins popped his head in now and again on his way to and from making sure all the SE kids were getting on okay.

'Done yet?' he asked for the third time.

'Not yet,' I said.

I had barely started the assignment. The book was open, and I kept starting to look for the answer to question two and then I would drift into thinking about the logistics of getting Chris from the school to the train station the next day. I was trying to remember if there was a lift on every bus that went past the school, or only on some of them. I would have to check out the bus schedule.

And just when thoughts of the craziness of the whole idea started to creep in, I would again feel the weight of my conversation with Mom that morning. I had wanted so badly for her to be okay this time. I had worked so hard for it. And for what? She didn't want to be normal, and worse, she wanted me to be unhappy.

And Chris *was* unhappy. My plan might be crazy, but at least it would be trying to help someone who actually might want help.

A few minutes later Mr Jenkins returned, but this time Dr Sharon was right behind him. My heart jumped. It was

Thursday, not our usual Monday meeting day. My first thought was that there was something wrong with Mom. Habit. I wondered if I would ever not have to worry about her. But then I remembered that it would be Francie that would be at the door if there was a problem with her.

'I have a few moments before I have to head off to another school,' Dr Sharon said, 'Is it okay if I talk to you now?'

'Okay,' I agreed, though I didn't feel like it was at all okay. I was kind of embarrassed by having stormed out of the room on Monday. Just seeing her now brought the confusion and anger back to the surface, adding to the hurt from my conversation with Mom that morning.

Dr Sharon assumed her usual position, relaxed but distant, across the table from me.

'I didn't want to leave it a week before seeing you, since we didn't finish our time together the other day.'

'I'm sorry I left,' I attempted to make our relationship tidy again, but it was getting harder and harder to put my feelings into the locked box I usually kept them in.

'Why sorry? You were upset.'

We just sat there a minute then. Dr Sharon always seemed completely at ease with silences. I, on the other hand, could never stand them, except with Chris. Chris was different of course because there had never been anything but silence from him in our friendship, but also because I never felt that he might be quietly judging me.

'It's not easy to just sit back and let someone be unhappy you know,' I defended, 'especially when it has probably been their whole life they've been unhappy.'

'I can see it's upsetting you.'

'Not anymore,' I divulged. 'Maybe nobody else cares, but I do. *I* won't just sit back.'

'You're very strong that way, Jo. Look at the difference you have made in Chris's life. He is lucky to have such an under-standing friend,' I was surprised to hear her say, 'and yet ... you have had to sit back and wait an awful lot in your own life haven't you?'

I wanted to let the tears come, I really did. I wanted to agree with Dr Sharon, to admit that I had waited my whole life for something to be better: for a break from always taking care of Mom, and yet never doing it well enough; for a friend that I could have come to my home; for a week without worry.

I couldn't risk crying now though. If I opened that box of feelings, I wouldn't have the strength to go through with my plan. Maybe I had failed in keeping things okay for Mom, but I wasn't going to fail Chris now – even if I didn't have a clue how I could pull it off.

'It's okay to ask for help,' she offered.

I was relieved when the bell rang and I could head off to second period, narrowly escaping crying on Dr Sharon's shoulder, which I thought surely would have ruined her expensive suit jacket.

When the lunch bell rang I was slow to head off to help Chris with lunch. For the first time since I had met him my heart just wasn't in it. Ironic. I'd never been more concerned for anyone as much as I was concerned for Chris right now. Yet I didn't really want to see him.

Things had been strained between us the last few days. He still wasn't smiling and I had been too distracted with trying to come up with some sort of plan to ask him many questions. I wouldn't let him down though. Besides, where else would I go?

I was in before Chris. He was a bit late. I put my head down and tried to calm the jumpiness of my stomach. Nothing seemed right anymore. My feelings were playing chase with my thoughts and it all seemed mixed up together. I was angry with Mom but I was sad about her too. I was sad for Chris, but I was scared too about actually taking him to the conference. Did I know what I was doing?

It had seemed so simple last night. Get Chris on a train. If it was so the right thing to do, why wouldn't my stomach stay still? Was I *truthfully* trying to help Chris – or was I using him as an excuse to escape myself?

Flo wheeled him in and I looked up, giving him as much of a smile as I could muster.

'He's been ready for lunch since this morning, I'd say. Every time I say your name his face lights up,' said Florence.

'He wasn't happy about our holdup waiting for the microwave to be free.'

Chris didn't seem to be smiling now though. He was looking at me with furrowed brows.

'Always glad to see you too, Chris,' I said, trying to feel like I meant it.

Florence left and I pulled out the book that Chris had been reading.

'No,' he indicated with his head.

'I don't feel like talking today, Chris, if that's okay.'

He didn't answer that.

So lunch was quiet, both of us reading, as Chris ate and I turned pages. When he was finished eating, I put the book down.

'Anything you want to say today, Chris?'

'Yes,' he indicated.

I took out the battered cards from my backpack, and laid them out. H O M E S A D Chris slowly spelled. Home. Sad. Tears came to my eyes and then when I looked at Chris, there were tears in his eyes too.

The medicine ball had been thrown at me again. There was only one thing I could do. Chris couldn't be clearer in his plea for me to help him.

'That's it. We're going.'

CHAPTER TWENTY-TWO

Looking back, I would not be able to believe that I headed out of the door of the SE wing without a single thought as to where we were going. But that's what I did. I just started walking, trying to manoeuvre Chris's chair as quickly as I could with his arms waving frantically in front of me.

It was only when we were in the main building that my heart began to race and I began to think of where we were going – if we made it out of the school.

I looked at my watch. We had about fifteen minutes before the end of lunch. There wasn't much time to inconspicuously stroll out of the school without being noticed. And it wasn't like Chris's big blue beast of a wheelchair helped us to blend in. As soon as Flo walked into the little room where Chris and I had shared lunch for two months and found Chris not there, the search would be on.

The hallways were much easier to get through than they usually were when I wheeled Chris to and from art though. It was a nice day, and most people were still outside. The farther we got from the SE wing the louder my heart seemed to beat. I sped up, expecting at every turn to be caught. We went around the last corner before the main door so fast Chris's chair was nearly on two wheels.

And nearly ran right into Sarah. Who I had been trying to avoid for two months.

I hadn't exactly *not* seen her all that time. It was a big school, but not *that* big. But when I had seen her, I had suddenly become very busy looking in the opposite direction, pretending that I hadn't seen her.

Now I couldn't avoid her. There wasn't even anyone else in the foyer. And I couldn't think of a worse time for it.

'We're late.' I blurted the first nonsense that made it from my brain to my mouth.

'Oh, well,' Sarah was out of words too. 'Anything I can go to with you?'

'No ... it's an appointment,' I managed before going on.

I practically ran outside into the bright sunlight.

We had to get far away quickly. I headed to the city bus stop two blocks away. The only bus line that I knew from here was the one that went to my suburb on the edge of town. I knew the buses ran every twenty minutes at this time of day, but I didn't know how often the wheelchair-accessible buses ran. All I could do was hope that a bus came soon and hope that it was a bus that Chris could get onto.

I found out right away that pushing Chris's chair in the school was a whole lot easier than outside. Some of the side-

169

walks had sloped sections to get on and off, but they were not always where I wanted to cross the street, and I had to backtrack a couple of times. I had to be careful when we came to dips and uneven bits as Chris's chair threatened to tip.

It seemed to be ages before we were at the bus stop, but when I looked at my watch there were still a few minutes before the end of lunch hour. I pulled the little levers to put the brakes on Chris's chair as Flo had taught me to do when I started to go to art class with him.

I hadn't said a word to Chris since leaving our room. Now I looked at him and gave a shaky smile. His face was drained of colour and his eyes were wide with fear. His arms and legs were still moving wildly.

'It's okay, Chris. I know what I'm doing,' I tried to reassure him, even though it was a complete lie. 'I *hate* that group home you live in. I'd cry every day if I had to live there.'

He was banging his head to the right repeatedly, 'No.'

'I'm listening. No more group home.' Seeing how upset he was helped me to calm down. 'Home sad' was the first real communication to me about how he felt about his own life. I was doing the right thing. Sure it was crazy, and I didn't know what we were doing, but anything had to be better than seeing Chris so unhappy.

I kept looking at my watch. The end of lunch bell would be ringing now. Where was the bus? What if it didn't come soon? I would give it five minutes and then I would have to come up with another plan.

But sure enough, the bus did barrel down the road in two minutes – and it was an accessible one, as I could tell as soon as the doors opened and the hiss of the hydraulics lowered it to sidewalk level.

I tried to appear casual as I went to drop the change for two fares into the fare box.

'You don't have to pay. Disabled companions go free with a Disability Card,' the bus driver said, covering the change slot.

'Oh ... yeah. I forgot,' I fumbled.

He didn't ask to see Chris's card; I supposed it was pretty obvious that he met the criteria, even if he didn't have a card.

I managed to flip one of the front benches up and was trying to figure out the straps to secure the wheelchair, but the driver came back to do that. He was slow and methodical in tightening everything and checking it again before returning to his driver's seat. Several people let out loud sighs of impatience with the delay. So much for being inconspicuous.

I glanced at Chris, wanting him to reassure me, but his eyes were turned down.

I looked around. Nine people. Not many people, but nine people who could identify us when the alarm bells were raised at school. There wasn't a chance that they would not notice us – well maybe the woman way at the back that didn't look up from her book, but certainly none of the rest.

Through all of this I was thinking. The conference did not start until tomorrow. I was still hoping for some miracle there, some sort of great place to go. In order to even have a chance to find Chris some better options, we had to disappear long enough for me to think through a plan.

There was only one option that I could think of. My cabin. We could go there to hide out until I had a plan. It would be tricky to get along the river bank, but it could be done. I knew every obstacle almost by heart. And who would look for us there? I didn't think very many people even knew it existed, and if they did, no one would guess I would bring Chris there.

Just in case though, I rang the bell two stops before the one closest to my house and even after we were off the bus I pointed Chris's chair in the opposite direction and started to walk that way until I was pretty sure there was nobody to see us. The houses along this stretch were set back from the road, with meandering expanses of lawn and surrounded by big cedar and spruce trees. Besides, there were no cars in any of the drives. The people who lived in these houses that backed onto the park along the river were probably mostly in offices downtown at this time of the afternoon.

My heart didn't stop thumping until we reached the almost hidden path that lead down to the river. There were dozens of these paths, most of them ending at the river bank. Nothing distinguished my path from the others, but I knew it with my eyes closed.

As soon as I steered Chris's chair off the road onto the path, I realised that it was totally different negotiating the path in a wheelchair though. I had never thought of the path as narrow. Sure, the ferns brushed my arms as I walked through in places, and I pushed through bushes in spots, but the path was never lost. Now though, Chris's chair only made it a few feet before hitting a barrier of leaves and branches. I pushed until his chair stopped moving forward, then went to the front of his chair and pulled until the branches gave way. I would just get us out of one tight spot and then we would come to another.

Even when we were on a relatively wide spot, the ground was treacherously uneven. Roots lurched out of the ground at unpredictable angles, threatening to launch Chris onto the ground. I had to inch his chair forward, ready to run to whichever side his chair threatened to tip over to, in order to set it back on four wheels.

It was exhausting. I was dripping with sweat by the time we reached the river bank. Well, by the time *I* reached the river bank – with Chris in tow. I had not had a chance to check in with him since we got off the bus. He was literally just a package until we could reach the cabin and I could pull out the cards so that he could let me know what he was thinking.

I just had to keep going. By the time we got to the river, I was realising how difficult it was going to be to get us to the cabin. This is where the path ended. It was only another kilometre or so downstream, but it was a tricky kilometre. I had always skirted along the riverbank, holding onto branches to swing around places where the trees came right down to the water. There was no way I could do that with Chris.

In the end I took off my shoes and socks, rolled up my jeans and waded into the water pushing Chris's chair. The bed of the river was full of big, rounded stones covered in green slime. It was very slippery, but at least the handles of the wheelchair gave me some stability. Still, the chair itself was not very stable as it bumped along into big holes and crevices between the stones.

The water was freezing, but I didn't even feel it once we started down the river. Just like on the path, I would push Chris's chair until it was truly stuck, and then I would go to the front to try to pull it out. Chris himself did not make it easy. He was flapping in panic. The river was pretty shallow, and his feet were well out of the water, but I imagined it must be pretty frightening to have no control, as your vehicle careens down a river.

'Almost there, Chris. Sorry about all this,' I said, trying to give him a big smile, which probably ended up more like a grimace. Chris had a look of terror pasted on his face. We *were* almost there. Just one more bend and we would come to the little sandy beach. I found some more strength to push him around the bend without getting stuck once. Just one final push and we would be there.

I'm not sure what happened next. One minute I was standing up, relieved that we had made it. The little beach was just ahead. The next minute I was down in the water. And Chris and his chair were on top of my right leg. Pain shot through my leg when I pulled it out and scrambled upright, but I barely noticed that in my panic to get Chris's chair out of the water. Somehow I managed to pull Chris, still strapped securely into the chair, onto the beach and then right the chair again. He was soaking wet, but at least he seemed otherwise all right.

It was only when I went to push him from the beach, across the little field to the cabin that I knew that I was not all right. My leg just wasn't working. I couldn't stand on it. I tried again. Shooting pain.

There was no choice though. The sun was almost behind the trees now. It would be getting cold soon. I had to get Chris inside and dried off. It was hard to stop from screaming with the pain. *One, two, three.* I concentrated on counting the steps to the cabin. I had pushed through pain before; at least this pain was tangible.

Sixty-one, sixty-two, sixty-three. We were there. But for the first time ever I did not feel the usual relief of arriving at my safe place. Instead cold, sharp fear gripped me. What had I done?

CHAPTER TWENTY-THREE

I managed to get Chris into the doorway of the cabin before collapsing on the floor beside him. I was feeling faint and shaky, but I knew that I couldn't give in to the feeling. I had gotten Chris into this mess and now I was the only one who could make sure that things did not get worse.

The first priority was to get him warm and dry. I was glad for the large pile of sticks and logs beside the fireplace. At least my anger at Mom over the last two days had motivated me to spend time doing jobs around the cabin. Besides foraging for the pile of firewood, I had aired out the blanket I kept there and had nailed an old board over a window whose pane of glass had completely fallen out. I had looked around the place in satisfaction yesterday when I was done.

Now I was seeing it through Chris's eyes – a tiny, decrepit cabin that should be knocked before it became a hazard. Boards missing from the floor, no toilet – even if I had been able to help him onto it – no heat, no stove or fridge. There was a scruffy old armchair and an old wooden table with a rickety chair. In the corner was an ancient single mattress, full of holes where mice had chewed it, on a rusty spring bed frame. It was a wreck of a place.

It would be better as soon as we had a fire going. I couldn't stand on my leg anymore, so I used my good leg and my arms to crawl crablike to the fire place and I got a small fire started. I avoided looking at Chris while I slowly fed small sticks to the flames, nursing the fire until it gained strength and I could start adding bigger logs that started to throw out a bit of heat. I didn't begin to know how I could make this up to Chris. At least he was calm, with his head hung down and his eyes averted from me.

I dragged myself over to him and holding onto his foot-rest, pulled his chair close to the fire. Every movement shot new pain through my leg and made spots swim in front of my eyes. I didn't care though. I had to get Chris warm. Then I dragged the blanket off the chair and pulled myself upright enough to tuck it around him as best I could, fighting the nausea that washed over me in waves.

'Are you okay now, Chris?' I finally asked him. He didn't look up at all.

'I'll get the cards out, okay?' I tried. 'I know you're scared, but we're going to be all right.'

I gave his shoulder a squeeze, wishing I knew this was true.

We needed the table for the cards and I couldn't move Chris from the fire which was just beginning to throw a little heat. So I was going to have to make another trip across the floor to pull the table near. Each foray was harder than the last. My leg was on fire. I needed to let Chris talk though, more for me than for him. Without his voice I felt utterly alone and scared for the both of us.

It wasn't until I had the table and the rickety chair pulled over that I realised my book bag was still on my back. Everything in it was soaking wet, adding to the weight. I had been dragging not just myself, but several kilos of books, across the floor. All of this without shoes and socks, which were probably floating down the river now. I definitely wasn't thinking straight.

Finally I was on the chair. The cards were also soaking wet. I had to carefully peel them apart. The ink had run, but I could still read them when they were laid out in front of Chris.

'Right. Now. Talk to me.' My voice came out sounding small and shaky, just the way I felt.

Chris would still not even raise his eyes to meet mine.

'Please, Chris!' I pleaded, blinking back the tears that were threatening to come. 'I can't do this without you.'

He still didn't move.

'I'm sorry. I didn't even have a chance to tell you my plan. Or to ask you.'

I paused again to see if he would engage with me. He wouldn't.

'I couldn't let you stay in that house. I have to find you people that care about you and that can help you *really* talk.

It wasn't supposed to go this way . . .' my voice trailed away. Now that I was saying it out loud, the whole idea seemed ridiculous. What way was it ever supposed to go?

'It's just that . . . I've never seen you cry. It's usually me.' I looked up at him again.

All of the air rushed out of me. This was not right. Chris's head had snapped back and his whole body was rigid and shaking. His eyes rolled back to reveal white, and frothy red foam was appearing at the corners of his mouth. He was having a seizure!

'No, Chris, no!'

Mr Jenkins had told me that this could happen. It did happen to Chris every couple weeks or so, but I had been lucky enough not to have seen it. Mr Jenkins had told me to record exactly when the seizure started and to make sure there was nothing around him that he could bang into and hurt himself. But that was all – because the next step was to call someone for help. There was special medication for him if the seizure lasted for more than five minutes. That was why it was so important for someone to start timing the seizure.

But who was I going to call to help here? My phone! I searched through my bag, frantically feeling for it. After what seemed like ages I found it, but it was dead. I tried to turn it on three times, but the water had obviously ruined it.

Chris was still shaking and there was nothing I could do. His wheelchair was rocking and I was afraid that it might topple over again, and I knew I wouldn't be able to stop it even if I tried. It seemed like the seizure was going on forever. Was it more than five minutes? I didn't even have a watch to know.

Finally he stopped shaking and slumped forward. Despite the excruciating pain, I hobbled to him and lifted his head. I had never known Chris's body to be so limber. His eyes were closed, but when I put my hand under his nose I could feel his soft, warm breath. I sighed in relief.

But now I had another problem. Chris was exhausted. I knew I had to get him onto the bed, and that was going to be difficult enough. But I needed to keep him warm and that meant somehow getting the heavy bed as near to the fire as I could.

Already it was starting to get dark. It had to be around 4.30. I knew it got pretty dark by five now. So I dragged myself to the cupboard where I kept a small battery-powered lantern. It didn't give much light, but at least Chris wouldn't be in total darkness while I worked on getting the bed near the fire. Then I stoked the fire again, before starting on the laborious job of inching the stubborn bed across the floor. It seemed to take forever, dragging first one leg and then another, zigzagging over to Chris.

He was still slumped over when I finally had the bed as near to the fire as I could get it, but now he was shivering. This was not good. I needed to get him onto the bed quickly and get some of his wettest clothes off him so that I could dry them by the fire. I knew that I had to be extra careful that he didn't fall on the floor though, because I would never be able to lift him off of it.

I had never had to figure out how Chris was held into his chair, or how one might go about getting him out of it. At school Florence took care of all of that. I struggled with how to free his shoulders from the blue padded bars that held them there, finally figuring out the release mechanisms that let me swing them to the sides. I then had to unsnap the multiple buckles that kept his torso and hips in place despite the never-ending movement of his body.

Suddenly I didn't have time to think about how I was going to get him onto the bed. He was slipping and I had to move fast. Sheer adrenaline and desperation drove me to lift him and fall backwards onto the bed. I couldn't help it; I screamed in pain as I briefly took all of Chris's weight on my legs. Something snapped. And then everything was black.

CHAPTER TWENTY-FOUR

When I woke up, I couldn't see anything at first. I didn't know where I was, but I knew something was very wrong. I was dripping in sweat and my right leg throbbed in pain.

Finally my eyes adjusted and I saw a small glow down below me. The fire. I remembered now. In a panic I sat up, feeling for Chris. He was there beside me so we had obviously made it to the bed. I felt for his face and could feel him breathing. Despite how hot I felt, I knew it must be cold in the cabin and I had to make sure that Chris was warm.

Slowly I raised myself to sitting. I couldn't remember ever feeling this weak. My whole body ached, but especially my leg. Feeling down my hurt leg, I could tell it had swollen to twice its size. It must be broken.

I was afraid to move the leg at all, but when I inched off the bed onto my good leg I was surprised to find that the excruciating pain I had felt when I moved it before was gone. Instead, my bad leg seemed almost disconnected from me.

When I got the fire going again, I could see that Chris was asleep. I wondered how long it had been that he had lain there awake, not able to even adjust himself to get more comfortable. Had he worried about me, lying motionless beside him?

What a mess I had made of things. Yesterday it had seemed so important to fix all of Chris's problems immediately. But all I was doing was risking his very life. I hadn't even thought about how I was going to take care of his physical needs. I was failing Chris just as much as I had failed my mom.

I wondered how Mom was doing right now. Our rocky week was enough to destabilise her; having me gone missing was going to be devastating. Not just missing, but kidnapping someone completely defenceless.

I hoped that somebody was with her to make sure she took her medication.

And then I remembered the woman at the group home going from kid to kid with the little cups of pills. There had been a ton of them for Chris. I didn't even know what they were for. How badly did he need those medications?

Here, in the dark, with every decision mine alone, I finally knew what I should have known all along. Dr Sharon was right. I couldn't do it all on my own. It didn't matter how miserable Chris was, living in the group home. I didn't have the solution to that problem. Maybe other people did. At least I could tell them what Chris had told me.

And I couldn't help Mom on my own either. I didn't want to.

Chris needed help. I needed help. It would have been a whole lot easier to ask for help the day before in the relative comfort of the school. Now I was going to have to literally crawl on my hands and knees to ask for it.

I waited until it was light to go. It was the longest night I had ever spent. The anxiety of the last week was gone with my decision to go for help, but I was terrified for Chris. I wasn't sure how quickly he needed that help.

All night I had kept getting off the floor to check him, each time afraid that he might not be breathing. It was cold, though I only knew that from feeling Chris's hands, which were as cold as ice packs. *I* felt like I could heat the room I was so hot. In between checking Chris and putting more wood on the fire, I drifted in and out of sleep, hoping for daylight every time I woke.

Finally I opened my eyes to a dull light making its way in the window that wasn't boarded up. I looked over at Chris and saw that his eyes were open, looking at me.

'I've never been so glad to see your eyes, Chris,' I whispered.

I gripped the seat of the wooden chair and pulled myself up enough to get my good leg under me to stand on it, using the backrest to stabilise myself. From there I could just reach the bed, shuffling on my good leg until I could sit on the edge of the mattress. It was the technique I had been using all night long.

In the weak light I could see that Chris's lips were blue. I reached for his hand. There was no response when I took it and it was pale and blue tinged too. This wasn't good. I had to go now. All I could do was hope that I could find help quickly and that Chris would hold on until then.

His eyes were closing again, so I didn't even know if he was aware that I was beside him.

'I'm sorry, Chris,' I apologised again. 'I'm going for help now. We're going to get help. I've screwed up, but trust me that I would never let you down on purpose. I'll bring someone I promise.'

He gave the briefest nod. I would have missed it if I wasn't so close to him. It was the most communication he had given me since the two words he had spelled to me the day before.

The rain started just as I was outside the door. It was a typical heavy, winter rain. In seconds I was soaked to the skin – again.

I had thought about the best way to get myself to the road while I stoked the fire for the last time before leaving Chris. I was not going to be able to hobble that far. My leg wouldn't take any weight, even if I could stand the pain. I was going to have to drag myself.

First I had stabilised my leg. I think I'd seen that on some movie or something. You had to keep a broken leg from moving. I had pulled two planks from the cupboard shelf. For once it was a good thing that every piece of wood was rotting. The boards willingly left the rusty nails holding them in place, trailing crumbling splinters behind them. Using the knife from my supply cupboard, I had then cut the straps off my backpack. With these I crudely tied the big splints onto my leg.

So now I was inching crabwalk backwards, moving one hand at a time, and then pushing off with my good leg. It was slow, but it was working.

I felt a bit like a husky dog pulling a big wooden sled, but at least the boards kept my leg kind of protected as I dragged it around bends and over branches along the narrow river-bank. What I had not thought to protect were the palms of my hands which quickly became red and raw from scraping on the rocks and sticks.

Each backward 'step' was a mission. Left hand back, right hand back. Bring my left foot to my bottom. Push off, rais-ing my body enough to move myself a few centimetres at a time. Wipe the streaming water out of my eyes so I could see again. Every ten pushes I gave myself a rest. My head felt foggy and my whole body weak. It was the thought of Chris, alone in the cottage that focused me though. I had to get help as soon as possible.

I came to the first place along the bank that was too narrow for my splinted leg, so I had to drag myself back into the water. I was soaked to the skin already, but the icy water quickly numbed my hands so that I couldn't feel the surface behind me. They slipped on the slimy rocks, plunging my shoulders into the freezing water. I struggled to catch my breath and to push myself backward back up to the bank.

I didn't know if I could do this. It was still so far and my arms were getting weaker. I just wanted to put my head down and stay right here. If it were not for Chris, I probably would have.

Ten more pushes. Rest. Ten more pushes. Rest. Slowly, I kept going. Around each bend in the water. Then onto the bank to inch along a bit further.

I cried in relief when I saw the opening in the forest that was the start of the path leading up to the road. I was going to make it. I knew I would.

I think it probably took me another hour to make it to the road. The rain had finally stopped and I emerged backward from the heavy canopy of trees to sunshine.

A running shoe flashed over me, landing beside my head.

'Hey!' a voice above me exclaimed in surprise.

'Help,' I managed. 'My friend needs help.'

CHAPTER TWENTY-FIVE

I heard voices. They seemed to be very far away. I tried to open my eyes, but they just wouldn't open. I didn't want to wake up yet. My thoughts were hazy and I couldn't bring them together to make sense. There was only this vague feeling that it was better to sink back into the dreamless place I had emerged from than to struggle out of it.

When I opened my eyes, there was another pair looking right back at me. It took me a minute to focus and comprehend that they were Mom's eyes.

I raised my head and looked around. I was in a bed with a pale green curtain pulled around it. Mom was beside me in a chair and her head rested on the bed, her hands folded under her chin.

'Welcome back,' she whispered.

'Where was I?' I felt confused.

'Places I will only dream of going,' she said.

It was slowly coming back to me now. Running from the school. The journey to the cabin. The fateful fall. The long night. The epic trip back to the road. Chris. Where was he?

'Where is Chris? Is he okay?' I hoped that I didn't have to

explain who he was.

'He's okay, Jo. Had the ride of his life I'd say,' Mom said. 'Paramedics picked him up in a helicopter.'

'I'm sorry, Mom. I screwed up,' I apologised. 'I guess I'm in pretty big trouble.'

'I don't think you can come close to matching me for screwing up.'

She reached over and gave me an awkward hug. I wished I could enjoy this rare contact, but my arms hurt too much. I thought of my leg, which strangely didn't seem to hurt, and tried to sit up to look at it. I couldn't seem to do it.

'Don't try that yet,' Mom said, finding the crank to raise the head of my bed. 'They have you on the heavy-duty drugs, and believe me I know all about them. You don't want to be moving too much.'

My head slowly rose with the bed and I could see what must be my leg now. It was raised on a pillow and it was huge. There was a long red line down my shin and metal bits poking out by my ankle. I reached out to touch it, but was stopped by a clear tube attached to the back of my right hand.

'Guess you have figured out by now that your running away days are over for a while,' Mom pointed out the obvious. 'It's broken in a couple of places. I was a bit disappointed that there's no plaster cast though. I was thinking we would be able to cover it with names of obscure authors.'

I managed a smile. The anger I had felt toward her was gone. It was good to hear her quirky comment.

She fluffed up a couple of pillows and set them on either side of me. Then she raised a plastic cup of water with a straw in it to my lips. I had never known her to be so mom-like. Only the slight shake of her hands and her eyes darting toward the curtain opening betrayed her usual nervous energy. When I dutifully took a sip, Mom sat down and took my free hand.

'I've been waiting for hours to talk to you. I have to say it, while I still have the nerve. Are you okay to listen to my rambling one more time?' she asked.

I nodded.

'I've been terribly afraid, Jo. The last couple of months I've seen you growing. I was afraid to lose you. You're always so strong, so capable. And you know I'm not. I don't cope very well. We both know I'm a total disaster.' She gave a bit of a laugh.

'Mom, it's okay, you're—'

She held up her hand, stopping me.

'No need, Jo. Let me go on.' She wasn't ranting, just quietly saying what she had obviously been preparing to say. 'I've used you so much to keep me centred. And it's not fair. These last couple of days, I've met people in your life I didn't even know existed – and they really care about you.'

Tears were streaming down Mom's face now. I wanted

to slip into my usual role of comforting her, making things okay, but she was gripping my hand so tightly, I couldn't move.

'I might not show it in the right ways, but I categorically love you. I did from the moment I felt you do your first back flip in my uterus. I don't want to trap you. I've talked to your grandma. If you want, you can go live with her. I'll let you go, Jo.'

'No, Mom!' Now I was crying too. 'I love that you're weird and spontaneous and just ... you.'

I meant it. As inconvenient, and difficult as it was at times, I was connected with her in a way that couldn't just be erased. I didn't want the suffocating safety of living with Grandma. But I knew now that I didn't want to be Mom's caretaker either. It was too much for me. It was too much for both of us.

'We need help. We never ask for it, but now we need to.'

Mom just nodded, fresh tears streaming down her face.

* * *

It was not until the next afternoon that I got to see Chris. I had spent the day before in and out of sleep, too foggy most of the time to think very clearly even in between doses of painkillers that knocked me back unconscious. But when I woke the next day, all I could think about was seeing with my own eyes that Chris was okay.

I wasn't sure that he would ever want to talk to me again though. Not only had I not been able to help him, but I had very nearly made things much worse. It seemed ludicrous now that I would have even considered it possible to just take him away to another city and find him some new life. How would I, on my own, have done that exactly? What had I even been looking for? During the long night in the cabin I had accepted that Chris might hate me forever for what I had done, and I had decided that it didn't matter as long as he was alive. Now I was ready to face my mistakes and that meant seeing Chris, at least to apologise and say goodbye.

As it turned out, that was not going to be so easy. I brought up the subject with the first nurse I saw, who came around at 6a.m. to check on me. It was all business in the hospital. First, my temperature was taken.

'Good. It's back to normal,' the nurse commented.

'What about Chris? I know he's here. Is he okay?' I asked.

'Well, I can't actually comment on that sweetie,' the nurse put me off, getting busy taking my blood pressure and checking the bag of fluids that flowed into my hand.

'But I need to know. I need to see him,' I insisted, fully awake and alert for the first time since waking up in my pale green tent.

'We have this thing called patient confidentiality,' the nurse explained. 'I can't tell you that someone else, who is not related to you, might be recovering just fine. Someone might have had moderate hypothermia, but luckily been taken to hospital in time because of another person's bravery, and I couldn't tell you that. I also wouldn't be able to tell you, just for example, if someone got very exited when they saw a picture of you on the news.'

My first reaction was to smile. I wanted to hug the nurse for her kind gesture. Then I processed the rest of the information – my picture on the news. I knew I could be in very big trouble at school for taking Chris away. But the news?

Apparently though, Chris and I disappearing hadn't exactly gone unnoticed. When Mom came in later that morning, she handed me the local Saturday paper.

'You didn't make the front page, but page two isn't such a bad effort,' she said.

I opened it to the second page. There was a picture of Chris – the one where he was painting, that had been in the brochure. Beside it was a picture of me – a bad school picture from the year before. Then there was a short article:

Happy Ending for Missing Teens

The mystery of the missing teen, Jo MacNamara, along with her disabled school mate Chris Fern, was solved yesterday when a jogger happened upon the girl while out for a morning run.

'I nearly stepped on her. You just don't expect to see someone lying on the path,' said Samantha Jones.

It seems that the pair had spent the night in the woods near Cedar Grove Estate after leaving Thorton Secondary in the early afternoon of Thursday. A bus driver on route 10 reported picking up the two at a stop near the school and dropping them at a stop in the estate.

'I didn't think about it at the time, but when I heard on the radio that they were missing, I remembered straight away that it was pretty unusual for a kid in a wheelchair not to have an adult with him,' said Joe Fielding.

The girl was taken to hospital, where she is in stable condition, recovering from non life threatening injuries. The boy was located about one mile away and airlifted to hospital. He too is in stable condition.

'When I found her, she was in pretty bad condition,' said Jones. 'She was bleeding pretty badly, and she seemed to be in shock. All she could say over and over again, was to find her friend, that he was in danger.'

It is still unclear why Jo would have taken Chris, a severely physically impaired fifteen year old. No other people are suspected to be involved, and as both are minors, no charges are expected to be laid. However, given the level of disability of the boy, the police have concerns about the teen girl endangering his life in what was essentially abduction.

'We are respecting the wishes of both the family of the girl and the care staff of the boy in their request to allow Jo to recover before questioning her,' said Officer Morgan.

It won't be possible to question Chris, as he is non-verbal and has no means of communicating.

'Wow, I think I *am* in trouble, Mom,' I said, when I had finished reading the article.

'You could say that you have stirred the pot of complacency, Jo.' Mom was as clear as ever. 'Newspapers don't always get the whole, or even the right, story. Notice the part about you being covered in blood? Not true. I was here to meet you before you went into surgery, a few scrapes on your hands, but other than that no blood.'

CHAPTER TWENTY-SIX

B ut in the early afternoon, sure enough a police officer did come to talk to me. The nurse came in and called Mom out, and then they both came in with the police officer, uniform and all. My heart sped up a little, but I thought back to the fear of being in the cabin, not knowing if Chris was okay, and knew that any trouble I was in didn't matter. Chris was alive and nothing else mattered.

Right away, the officer let me know that he was not here on a social visit.

'Hello, young lady,' he greeted me. 'I suppose you know that you are very fortunate that everything has turned out as it has.'

I nodded, holding tight to my confidence that everything would be okay.

'It is a very serious offence to take someone, or hold someone, against their will. You are only lucky that juvenile law applies to you, but consequences can still be serious. Do you understand what I'm saying?'

Again I nodded.

'Is it okay if I ask you a few questions?' the officer asked, taking off his hat.

'Yes. I'm ready,' I said, prepared to share everything.

He took out a small notepad and a pen.

'So I understand from Mr Jenkins that you were assisting Chris at lunch time on Thursday. But at the end of lunch, when Florence came to collect him, you were both gone. Can you take me through what happened?'

I took a breath and then just told him the whole thing. I started with Chris's communication: H O M E S A D and my sudden decision to run with him. I told him the details of getting to the cabin, the fall, the seizure, the fear that Chris might be very sick and even die. I just spilled out the truth.

The officer's expression didn't change through my lengthy retelling. He just nodded in encouragement. When I was done, he flipped back through the notes he had taken while I talked.

'You mentioned that Chris told you that he was sad at home, and that this prompted you to make the decision to run away. Can you explain that a bit? Chris can't talk, from what I understand.'

'He can't talk with his voice. And he's a bit stubborn, so he never wanted to use picture symbols to talk and that's what people were trying to teach him when he was a young kid. But somehow he learned to read, and his spelling isn't great, but he can dictate messages.'

The officer wasn't writing notes anymore. He was looking

at me with his mouth open.

'And you know this because?'

I didn't think he believed me at all.

'We have a way of talking. Can you show me your cell phone?'

I explained to him how Chris tapped his head, the same way someone would use the number pad to write a text.

'Why doesn't anyone else know about this? It's the first I heard he could communicate.'

'Because I'm stupid and thought I had to sort Chris's whole life out before I let anyone know,' I supposed. And there was more. 'Plus, I think it was that I thought it was something special that only I could talk with Chris. In a way I didn't want to share that. I thought I could be the one to make everything perfect, and I just couldn't. That was wrong, and selfish.'

'So if I went in to ask Chris questions, he could answer me?' the officer asked.

'If he wanted to he would. I can't promise he will.'

'And tell me, I had down that Chris is, how do you say…' He flipped through his notes again, finding an underlined bit. 'Intellectually impaired, probably in the moderate range? Are you saying that isn't true?'

I smiled, remembering a similar conversation with Mr Jenkins.

'I don't know. Does it matter? It's not like someone who

isn't as smart, or even isn't able to use words to talk, can't let you know how they feel. You just have to listen.'

* * *

I sat clutching the pieces of torn paper, with their hurried letters scrawled on them. I had shown the officer how to use the system, mimicking the way that Chris would respond with his head while the officer practised by asking me questions. Then I had pleaded to see Chris, just for a short while, and to explain to him that someone new was going to use the communication system to ask him questions.

'He just might be more likely to talk to you, if I set it up first,' I tried. 'That is, if he'll ever talk to *me* again.'

'I suppose so. But I'll leave it to the nurse to make sure he's okay with seeing you,' he had warned.

So now I was being wheeled to see him. He was in a room just down the hall. There were three other beds in the room, but all of them were empty. The head of Chris's bed was propped up and he was hooked up to an IV much the same as the one the nurse wheeled along with my wheelchair. I was relieved to see the smile I was used to seeing on his face.

'Remember, only five minutes,' the nurse reminded me, as she parked my wheelchair nearby – too far for me to reach Chris's bed. I was learning what it was like to rely on someone else for movement.

'Is it okay for you to bring me right up to Chris? We need

these cards to talk, and I need to put them on the bed.' I indicated the pieces of paper in my lap. I saw the nurse hesitate. 'It's not like I can do a runner out the door with him now.'

The nurse smiled and inched my chair right beside him and then headed out the door. I took a deep breath and looked Chris in the eye, hoping he would know how sincere my next words were.

'First, I'm so sorry, Chris. I didn't mean to scare you. I didn't mean to drop you in the river and I understand if you will hate me forever.' I had practised these words on the way down the hall.

'Do you hate me?' I asked, prepared for him not to answer. He did though, a definite head tap to the right, 'No.'

'I only have a few minutes, and then the police are going to ask you questions. So, it's up to you, anything you want to say to me?'

He tapped to the left.

'Okay. I'm going to listen this time.'

Chris had never been so definite and fast in his head tapping. N O T M E S A D J O S H O M E S A D. Then he stopped responding.

It took a minute for me to figure out the words. Then I did and I understood my mistake.

'Not me sad. Jo's home sad,' I read out. 'Is that right, Chris?'

An emphatic 'yes'.

Chris had not been telling me that he was sad in his own

home; he had been worried about *me* and the problems I had in *my* home. I had misread him completely. Presumed that he *must* be sad to live in the group home. During all my rambling every lunch hour I had thought I was just talking to myself. But Chris had been carefully listening to me, really caring, even knowing I was sad without me even talking about it.

Even though we only had a few minutes together, I had to just sit and take that in before I prepared him to talk to the police. I didn't have any experience in having a friend. It had never occurred to me that Chris might be sad for *me*. It was the strangest thing – knowing that he cared that I had been sad, suddenly made me happier than I had ever been.

But it wasn't the time to tell him any of this. The nurse was back to take me to my room. I had to let Chris know about his next conversation – if he chose to have it.

'I'm only allowed to be here a few minutes, and I think the time is up,' I said, nodding my head toward the nurse. 'There is a police officer here, and I've showed him how we talk. He wants to ask you about me taking you from the school.'

Chris's eyes were intently on mine, and his brows furrowed.

'Please, Chris. Talk to him. I don't care what you say. Just … it's your first chance to talk to someone, and he's promised he'll listen.'

That's all that I had time for. The nurse wheeled me away and the police officer walked in to Chris. I wasn't worried. Whatever he said was going to be okay. As long as he chose to say *something*.

I knew that Chris could be stubborn when he wanted to be, but I should have known by now that he also seized opportunity when it came along. The officer had promised that he would give me an honest report of how it went, as long as it was okay with Chris, if he said anything at all. It was nearly an hour later when he returned, still carrying his little notepad.

I looked at him expectantly, half dreading what he might have to say to me. He was shaking his head when he sat down and I felt my face drain of colour. I was in trouble.

'I've a lot to report back to you,' he said. 'Chris had a lot to say it seems. I didn't exactly think you were lying about him talking to you, but I didn't believe he would say so much. He wants me to tell you all this by the way.'

The officer opened his notepad.

'This was his response to my question about being taken from the school by force. And I quote: Surprised, but I trust Jo. She my friend. Only wants to help me. Nobody listened before. Gives me a voice, first time ever. Please don't put her in jail. I need her. Everything okay with us. No jail please.'

'He said that?' I was incredulous. Chris had never been able to say that much before.

'And you are right. His spelling is atrocious. Took me ages to get it right.'

I wouldn't get to speak to Chris for nearly two weeks. He was released from the hospital the next day but I had to stay and it would be two weeks before I was finally able to go back to school on crutches.

A lot happened in that time though. And when I saw him next, it would never be just me and Chris talking again. Chris would be able to talk to anyone he wanted to.

When Mr Jenkins came to visit me the next day it almost seemed like I was back in science class with him. He popped his head in my hospital room door, without actually entering the room, much the same as he would have in the SE wing.

'You missed science Friday, so I thought I might stop in and pick up our lesson here,' he teased, 'Unless you're busy?'

'Actually, you are one on my long list of apologies to be made,' I said.

'Oh good,' he said, striding in the room and sitting down for once. 'But apologies are all mine I'm afraid – though I do admit that I wasn't so happy with you a couple of days ago.'

'Sorry about that. I know the police were around and everything. Was it bad?'

'Typical teens going missing hardly registers, I'm afraid. Kids in our wing, now that's a different story. S-h-i-t hits the fan,' he said. 'We had a lot to answer for, but hey, it's all in a day's work.'

'I understand if I can't help Chris anymore.'

'Well, I have a feeling we will be able to work through that one. But first my apologies.'

'For what?'

'I wasn't upfront with you, Jo, and I'm afraid I probably contributed to you feeling you had nowhere to turn.'

'What?' I wasn't sure what he was talking about.

'I've just been in to see Chris and one of his house staff. They had no idea before now that Chris was opening up to anyone. They're pretty excited about it, by the way.'

'They know about that now? And I guess you do too,' I said, feeling my face flush at hearing our secret revealed.

'They do after one amazed police officer paid them a visit. Me, on the other hand, I had a fairly good idea that you two were up to some kind of communicating quite a while ago. I didn't push you to share it with me, because I secretly hoped you were the key to unlocking the potential I suspected all along,' he confessed.

'You did?' I was surprised. Wasn't he always trying to dissuade me from thinking Chris had more capability than he showed? 'But I thought you didn't care at all.'

'I see that now, and for that I'm sorry. Really I am,' he

apologised again. 'I'd tried for two years to get him to communicate. I'd see a spark of interest sometimes, and I could see Chris follow conversations when he was interested, but mostly he'd just go into another zone with me.'

'Mr Jenkins, he's very stubborn. Don't feel bad, he does that with me sometimes too.'

'Yes, but he *wants* to talk to you. I kind of used you, looking for a way – any way – to get Chris to want to talk.'

'That's okay. I guess it worked for me as much as Chris. Neither of us had anyone we wanted to talk to before now.'

'To be honest, I was so focused on finding the key to helping Chris communicate – I forgot that he just might not want to talk,' Mr Jenkins went on. 'I *should* have thought about it. I can't go into it, sensitive information about students and all, but he didn't have the easiest of childhoods before living where he does now.'

'I kind of know about difficult childhoods myself.' Somehow it didn't feel like betraying Mom anymore to say this.

Mr Jenkins was quiet for a moment.

'Maybe that's why he picked you, Jo. The rest of us were so busy trying to help him. For the first time someone needed *his* help.'

'No wonder he *stopped* talking to me then.' I smiled, thinking how true this probably was.

'I was planning to talk to you Friday because I was heading off to an important conference that afternoon. It was all about communication technology and I wanted to ask you if you thought there was anything that might benefit Chris.'

I started. Surely it was the conference that I had been wildly planning to take Chris to!

'I very nearly missed it too. We were gearing up for search parties on Friday morning and so going to the conference was the last thing on my mind. I managed to get to it on Saturday after you were found, though.'

'I can tell you what Chris needs. I can show you from the catalogues,' I began, and then checked myself. 'Well, I can tell you what I think – but you better ask Chris, not just me.'

'Good point.'

'It's just that everything is so expensive.'

'Yes, I won't kid you. That's a problem. I promise you that it is a problem I will tackle though. I'll find a way to get it for him.'

Mr Jenkins wasn't the only visitor I had that day. I was intent on trying to lean as far as I could to reach a book on my bedside table that was just out of reach, when a hand appeared and brought the book over to me.

'Here let me help you.'

I looked up to see Sarah. She smiled shyly as she handed me the book.

'Is it okay that I'm visiting you?' she asked.

'Sure,' I said, 'Are you sure you want to be around me though?'

'I never didn't,' Sarah said. 'I didn't know Lisa was such a cow, I swear I didn't. She is so mean, and she made it seem I said things I never said. The very next day after you ran out of lunch in the drama room I told her I didn't want to hang out with her.'

'Really?' I was shocked.

'I tried to stop you for weeks after that to explain, but you didn't even seem to see me, and then I just thought you must truly hate me. Maybe you still do.'

I was through with being afraid of what anyone thought of me. I didn't want to keep any more secrets, or try to fit in. I liked Sarah a whole lot, but if it meant trying to pretend that I lived a normal life, so that she liked me, then it wouldn't be worth it.

'Look, Sarah. I have to let you know. Lisa is right. My mom has some pretty serious mental health problems. That freaks people out. And we don't have much money; that's true too. But I'm not ashamed and I don't need sympathy.'

'Well, my dad is an alcoholic, and we had to leave him this last summer. And I *am* kind of ashamed of all that. Plus, with moving and all I don't know anyone, and I need a friend!' Sarah blurted out.

'Oh!' I exclaimed, 'I'm sorry Sarah, I didn't know. I'm just not that used to people wanting to be my friend!'

'I don't know anything about that. All I know is that you're funny and smart and I'd ten times rather have you as a friend than Lisa.'

'Well, I can see your point there,' I had to agree. 'She is kind of a cow.'

And the visitors didn't stop there. My final visitor that day, Mom's social worker, came for more serious reasons though.

'Here's the deal, Jo,' Francie started, without as much as a hello. 'I had to work my connections, but you seem to have done your part in impressing the cops as well. So some decisions have been made as to what to do with you.'

I waited for Francie to take off her coat and sit down.

'These situations could become very messy when there is history – not yours, but your mom's history.'

'What exactly do you mean by "these situations"?'

'Abducting a person, holding them against their will, endangering their life; that sort of situation,' Francie said.

'Oh, that.'

'Anyway, I've arranged for the group home supervisor and your school counsellor to meet with you tomorrow. It's going to have to be here, because you aren't going anywhere until the end of the week. All going well with that conversation, the whole matter will be dropped.'

'That's okay,' I approved. I just wanted to get the apologies over with now.

'There's more though,' Francie continued. 'I've talked with your mom, and this little stunt of yours just proves that you guys need more than me stopping in for a chat every once in a while. And it seems the stubborn pair of you may actually agree with me for once?'

'I love my mom, Francie, but I don't think I want to be the one to keep her sane anymore. You know what? I don't even think I can.'

It was such a relief to say that out loud. I could feel where that saying *taking a weight off your shoulders* came from, because I literally felt the weight shift.

'Well hallelujah for that! And lucky for you, resources being as tight as they always are, you went and scared the bejesus out of everyone. It's doing things like that that gets you moved right up the wait list. You just won your mom a community mental health nurse – coming soon to your house five hours a week!'

* * *

The meeting with the group home staff was scheduled for 10a.m. on Monday. The nurse had helped me into the wheelchair and wheeled me into a small room filled with sofas where I was expecting Dr Sharon and Mary from the group home. I wasn't expecting three other group home staff. Along with Mary, Cynthia walked in and two others who I had not met. Like Alison, who I had met when I went to the group home, they were youngish, and didn't scare me as much as Mary and Cynthia. They introduced themselves as Trisha and Julie, smiling politely, but saying nothing more while they perched expectantly on their chairs, waiting for Dr Sharon.

We had to wait another ten minutes, as Dr Sharon – characteristically casual – walked in late, taking her time to get out her note pad and pen before addressing the group.

'Welcome all,' she started. 'I'm a school psychologist for the district, and Jo and I have been doing some work together for the last couple of months. My job here today apparently is to facilitate a conversation between all of you. We'll see if we can all be on the same page by the end of our session. So, Mary would you like to start by letting Jo know the impact of her actions?'

Mary held a piece of paper in front of her and her hands shook slightly.

'It was just really hard to believe when we found out Chris was gone. The worry that night was unreal. We were worried about his medications being missed, if he was going to get to use the toilet, about how you would know what he needed.'

'The big question that night was why. Why would someone take Chris?!' Julie exclaimed.

'Can you answer that, Jo?' Dr Sharon directed the question to me.

'Yes. I'll try,' I said quietly. 'See, Chris isn't just someone I help out with at school. He is my friend, maybe my first ever real friend. It started out with him listening to me. I didn't know if he could understand what I said, but it was just so easy to talk to him.'

I looked up. All eyes were on me, listening.

'And then I found out he could read. Not just small words either – but whole books. And then we figured out a way for Chris to talk to me. The police officer told you that, right?'

'He did. I've told everyone and we want to know all about it!' Trisha said excitedly, and then looking around added with less enthusiasm, 'That is, after we're finished this part.'

'I've thought about it a lot, and I think I should have trusted people then, and told Mr Jenkins about Chris talking. I should have told all of you at Chris's house too,' I went on, 'But then I saw how Chris lives. It's so busy and there isn't time for talking ... And I'm sorry if I'm wrong for saying it – but it can't be right for someone not to even have the door closed when they're going to the toilet!'

'So you thought it might be better to take Chris into the woods? How exactly were you able to help Chris in a better way?' Mary shot back.

'I think what Jo might be saying, is that she felt for her friend, from the life perspective of a thirteen-year-old. Not that she even thought as far as having any answers,' Dr Sharon interjected.

I nodded gratefully.

'I was wrong. You're right, I couldn't look after Chris. But I thought Chris was asking me to take him away. He said, "Sad, home." But he meant me,' I admitted. 'He meant I was sad in my home. He was kind of right.'

'Okay. As long as we have that established,' Mary admonished.

'But I know you're right too about what you say,' Trisha said. 'Everyone has a right to dignity. We forget that sometimes.'

'But you didn't see it all, Jo,' Mary defended, 'I hope you'll come back again. I promise to listen to any suggestions you have about how we can improve things. But you have to promise to stay around long enough to see the good things about Chris's home.'

'Okay, it's a deal,' I smiled, relieved that I wasn't going to be shut out of Chris's life.

'So! Can we finally move on to Jo teaching us how to talk to Chris? I'm dying to know!' Trisha exclaimed.

'Anyone have a cell phone?' I asked. Four phones were raised immediately.

CHAPTER TWENTY-EIGHT

I t was the second newspaper article that changed every-thing. A reporter had come by to ask me questions early the next week, when I was still in the hospital. She wasn't allowed to speak to me without Mom's consent though, and Mom had point-blank refused.

'I will not have my daughter flaunted as some allegory of the society we live in!'

As usual, I hadn't a clue what she had been talking about, but I was kind of glad not to have to talk to anyone else. I had had quite enough people in my life to explain my actions to, without adding a stranger to that list.

It turns out the reporter was still able to get her story, though, as Mom pointed out an article on the bottom of the front page when she came in the next morning.

'Now that's better, Jo. Page one this time,' Mom said matter-of-factly. 'Not that I approve of this sort of publicity mind you. I think you'll be pleased though.'

I took the paper, eyes drawn to the article near the bottom.

In Search of a Voice

The curious case of a thirteen-year-old girl who disappeared with her severely-disabled peer last week has become clearer this week. It seems that there was more going on with the pair than anyone could possibly guess.

The lead investigating officer was astounded when he interviewed the young girl, and was told that the disabled boy she absconded with would be able to give his account of events that occurred late last week, despite the fact that he had no known way of communicating with words and was believed to be too intellectually disabled to do so.

'The guy can't talk. But this young girl said he would be able to spell out, letter by letter, answers to my questions. I have to say I was pretty sceptical. Kids in trouble can come up with the most elaborate lies,' said Officer Morgan.

It turns out she was right. While no one else in Chris Fern's fifteen years had ever found out that he could read, write and use those skills to communicate, Jo MacNamara somehow discovered that indeed he could.

'We look after Chris every day,' said Mary Saunders, supervisor at the home for disabled children where Chris lives. 'We know him better than anyone. But we never knew he would be capable of this. All of a sudden, he has things to say to us that we never imagined. It is going to change his life, and ours.'

The pair of teens had apparently been 'talking' for weeks, based on a system modelled simply on the number pad texting system employed by classic cell phones. Using this crude communication tool, Chris was able to tell the police officer that he held no bad feelings toward Jo for absconding with him, even though he was later hospitalised after suffering hypothermia and dehydration.

We spoke to his teacher, Bernard Jenkins, to find out his views on the student he has taught for over two years. Jenkins was instrumental in coordinating a search party for the pair that included Jo's family, Chris's long-term carers and concerned fellow students and community members.

'Chris is one of many who deserve a means of communicating,' he said. 'Jo knows that, and as a young person not yet jaded into accepting the practical limits, she is one of the only people Chris has trusted to ask for this basic right.'

When asked what he thought Chris needed he said, 'The only thing needed now is a proper system for Chris to use. In this day and age Chris should have access to technological tools that you and I take for granted. Unfortunately, there just isn't the five grand in the school's budget for the equipment he needs. And as a ward of the state, it's not like he has any family that are going to step up to the plate either.'

I didn't know whether to be pleased or upset. It was great that there was interest in talking to Chris. But it didn't sound like Mr Jenkins was any closer to getting Chris the equipment he needed, despite his promise to ensure he got it.

*　*　*

I didn't have to go back to school that week. Or the next. I was slowly getting used to relying on others for even the simplest things, like getting from the bed to the wheelchair. It gave me an appreciation of what Chris experienced every day of his life.

I was finally let out of hospital though the following Monday. That morning both Mom and Grandma came to take me home. I was going to be confined to a wheelchair for a while, at least until the surgeon was happy enough with my leg healing to let me begin to use crutches. Grandma had decided that if she couldn't take her granddaughter home for good, maybe she could handle living with her daughter for a week or so to help out.

'I suppose if the pair of you needs me I could just about manage another trip west,' she had said to me on the phone a few days before. I would never know how the conversations had gone between Grandma and Mom about who would have guardianship over me. Something had changed though, and both of them seemed more settled in how we all fit together as a family.

'Shall I bring the car to the door, Sue?' Grandma asked when I was settled in the wheelchair, for once consulting

Mom about anything at all.

'Such a nice day, maybe we'll just walk the twenty kilometres home!' Mom exclaimed, and when she saw Grandma stand slightly more erect, said quickly with a smile, 'I'm joking of course Mom! Yes, bring the car around, thanks.'

So, it wasn't like in the movies when everything between us was instantly perfect, but it was better and for once I was going to enjoy it while it lasted, for as long as it lasted, instead of worrying about when it would end.

It was a couple of days later, that I heard a shout from the kitchen. It was just after ten in the morning, and both Mom *and* Grandma had agreed that it was no harm for me to spend leisurely mornings in bed. Since Mom was camped out on the sofa, giving her own bed up to Grandma, she was now up before me for the first time since I could remember.

So it was Mom who rushed into my room with my new best friend – my wheelchair on loan from the hospital.

'Let's get you in this contraption. I think you may want to see this.'

'What is it, Mom?'

'Just help me get you in this chair before you miss your Grandma being human. I don't think I've seen her so animated since I took her to see that Broadway musical, I don't remember the name, that one she loves. It was years ago. I haven't seen her smile like this since then, anyway!'

I was wheeled into the kitchen before I was fully awake.

Then Grandma shoved the newspaper into my hands, pointing to a small article that she had circled in red.

A Voice at Last

In a dramatic conclusion to the unfolding story of Chris Fern and Jo MacNamara that we have been following since the two disappeared from Thorton Secondary nearly two weeks ago, Chris will finally have a means of communicating easily.

'I met John Smith, a representative from TechnaSpeak, a new technology firm specialising in making computer technology accessible, in a conference I attended just after Chris and Jo were found,' said Bernard Jenkins, a teacher of both Chris and Jo. 'He was keen to hear about Chris's needs, but at the time I didn't know exactly what they were. I took his card, and I thought that was the end of it.'

It was only the beginning though. It seems that when Smith read about Chris in this paper, he couldn't stand by and see Chris's needs go unmet.

'Chris is the perfect candidate for the adaptations we design,' says Smith. 'We're a new company, and to be honest, Chris is the best person to advertise just how much our products can do to adapt mainstream computer hardware and software to meet individual needs.'

Smith has donated equipment that will allow Chris to operate any computer with his eyes. Software designed specifically for Chris, will allow his typed words to be spoken immediately.

Not to be outdone, the national computer chain Compu-World has given Chris a laptop and a handheld device to pair with the special equipment and software donated by Tech-naSpeak. 'Upgrades will be available to Chris whenever he requires them,' said John Sanderson, manager of the Hillcrest branch of CompuWorld.

And what did Chris have to say, as he trialled his new voice? His message was simple, addressed to his close friend who inspired everyone to ensure Chris could talk. 'Get well soon, Jo. And bring the shepherd's pie!'

'Do you see that, Jo? That's my shepherd's pie he's talking about! And here I thought you were taking all that food I made to a stray dog!'

I couldn't wait to go back to school and talk to Chris. We had a lot to talk about.

EPILOGUE

I wheeled Chris into the classroom, to the desk that was set up for him. His desk had to be one of the ones on the far right because the power outlet was on the wall nearest to his desk. It was one of the glitches that Chris and John and I were working on concerning Chris's 'tech' as Chris and John called it. Without a power cord, Chris's laptop never lasted long enough. But I had ensured that he wasn't stuck at the back at least, even though that had been the English teacher's first choice. We had had enough of the back of the room in art.

This was Chris's first normal academic course without Florence. After Christmas, when I had begun advocating for him to attend more mainstream courses, English was the obvious first choice.

'So what do you think of trying out English?' I had asked him one lunch hour.

'I speak English,' Chris had replied, trying out yet another voice that John had set up for him. Chris apparently had not been happy to have any old male voice speak the words he typed with ever faster speed. He kept telling John that the voice wasn't right; it wasn't him. Ever obliging, John would go away and return with more voice samples for him to try.

'Ha, ha, Chris,' I had replied, and then realised that he might be serious. The more Chris had been able to talk, the more I had come to see how little he knew about almost everything. His life had been limited to what had been brought to his vicinity since he was born, and not that much had been brought to him apparently.

'I mean, taking a course about books and poems and plays.'

'Books. Okay. That's good,' said Chris's voice, taking longer than he would have liked. That was another thing he kept asking John to improve.

'Well, and writing too,' I added, going on to tease, 'Maybe the teacher can do something about your atrocious spelling!'

I set up Chris's laptop for him, making sure the inconspicuous dot on his forehead that acted as a signal so that he could use his eyes as a mouse, was securely in place. Then I hobbled to my own seat next to him.

My leg was still healing after eight weeks, but at least I was using a walking cast now, so I could go back to assisting Chris in Art and helping out more at lunch. Even when I had been on crutches I had spent lunch hours with him and there were often three of us now. Sarah had decided to join us for some lunch hours, when she didn't have a rehearsal. It turns out one good thing had come out of her brief friendship with Lisa. Sarah had landed one of the main roles for the play to be put on in the spring.

She liked to entertain us with her impersonations of certain of her fellow cast members.

'Honestly, you wouldn't believe how seriously some of them take themselves!' she'd said the other lunch hour. 'Sandra-Lynne, who by the way, will *not* answer to just Sandra, was, like "I'm soooo exhausted from all the revision I have to do each night. I have soooo many more lines than all of you".'

Chris had smiled the wide smile he used to reserve for me alone. I didn't mind though. Sarah balanced our friendship out with her calm, accepting nature. She had been instantly comfortable with Chris – flailing limbs, big blue chair, and all. And when Chris was in a stubborn mood, or when bleakness overtook my vision, Sarah had a way of bringing us out of ourselves without either of us even knowing it. I'd thought having one friend was great; having two was heaven. It turns out three people can be friends after all!

Chris and I had arrived to class early, because he had insisted we leave the SE wing in plenty of time so there was no chance he would be late. He wanted his laptop set up and ready before the last bell rang. Now kids were pouring in noisily and I could tell that he was either excited or nervous because his arms and legs were moving everywhere.

'Are you okay, Chris?' I asked.

He tapped to the left with his head, indicating 'yes'. Sometimes our trusty old system for yes or no worked better than even the best of tech. It's the system that Chris's house staff still used the most when things were busy in the house, and even that was helping them to listen to Chris now.

When Chris had gone home from the hospital, before he knew he was going to get his equipment, they had made the same mistake I had – thinking to use symbols to help him communicate. He had refused of course. The next time someone sat down with our system he had given them an 'earful' – an even longer 'text' than the police officer had gotten.

It was the first thing I was shown when I visited Chris at his house. Alison had written it down on card – with corrected spelling and grammar – and gotten it laminated, so that any new people would know how he felt.

Don't show me symbols. I won't use them. I HATE using the picture exchange symbols. When I was eight I picked a car symbol. The teacher asked 'Did I want a car ride? Did I want to go home?' I WANTED to say I had seen the coolest 1960s Ford Mustang that morning, but I wasn't sure if it was a '68 or '69 – could she show me a book where I could find out? The day I can say this with a symbol is the day I'll use them.

True to our deal, I had spent more time at Chris's house, and while I still thought it wasn't a place I would want to live, I was starting to see that Chris didn't mind it as much as I would have.

'Do you want to watch this channel, Chris?' Mary had asked after dinner the last time I had been over. She had wheeled him over to his routine spot by the television. When he had indicated 'no', she had flicked through nearly twenty more, with Chris saying 'no' to all of them, before I had interrupted her.

'Maybe, Chris, do you want to do something else?' I had asked, and he had indicated 'yes'. 'I'll get your computer and you can tell Mary what you want.'

Mary's slightly impatient sigh gave away just how happy she was to oblige Chris in the middle of a busy evening where kids needed to be bathed, lunches had to be readied for the next day, and medications needed to be administered. Some things were unlikely to change.

Still, the fact was that Chris needed people who could take care of all those kinds of needs. I had learned the hard way just how complicated his physical needs were. Chris had helped me understand how he felt one day at lunch, when I half jokingly criticised his home life.

'Any great conversations last night or was it the cartoon channel as usual?' I had asked.

He had frowned at me and then spent ages on his computer writing something, not pointing his eyes to the 'speak' icon until he was finished.

'It's not fair, Jo. I feel safe home. My body, it's not easy. They know without asking what makes me more comfortable. Even you don't know that,' Chris's electronic voice, several versions of voices ago, had spoken.

Plus, I could see that his home staff did really care about him. They tolerated me hanging out and giving hints about how to treat him didn't they? I had even been invited to go to Chris's next group home planning meeting, which apparently was about discussing what things he might want to do or plan for in the next six months. It would be the first meeting where he would actually be able to tell everyone what he wanted.

The teacher came into class and had us take out the novel we were reading. Chris was joining the class when we were in the middle of a book, but I had prepared him for that as well, with John's help. He had an e-format of the novel loaded on his computer, so that he could read it without anyone needing to turn the pages for him. He had read the whole thing already, even though he only had to read the first half.

'Okay, so, Jason, will you pick up reading the first page of chapter eight please,' the teacher said.

I tried to pay attention, but I had already read this chapter too. My mind drifted as Jason read. I smiled to myself, thinking back to Freddie, Mom's community nurse, coming by the night before.

'Hello!' he had called out as he knocked and then bounced into the house without being invited. 'How are my favourite girls?'

He always greeted us like this. I had come into the kitchen, just to see what he was wearing. I had never met someone with so many clothes, all of them brightly coloured and slightly wacky. Yesterday he had had on a pair of red flared pants and a matching red suit jacket. The topper was his purple bow tie, atop his only plain piece of clothing, his white shirt.

Freddie had started to come by our house when I was still in the wheelchair. His weird exterior had immediately put Mom at ease, and his easygoing sense of humour could soften even her most intense days. Usually he came by three times a week, but he had assured us both that he would come over more often if Mom hit a rough patch.

'This is how it works, girlfriends,' he had explained on his first visit, snapping his long, brown fingers. 'My job is to bring the sunshine when the clouds get thick. How much sunshine you need, depends on how dark the sky is.'

Yesterday could have been one of the really dark days. I had come home to find Mom still in bed. Usually I would have spent the evening alternating between trying not to disturb her and worrying that I should be getting her up. Instead, I had just called Freddie and he had come over an hour later.

'So where is that mother of yours?' Freddie had mocked. 'Shall I kick her lazy ass out of the bed?' He had knocked on her bedroom door and then waltzed in.

And I had stayed right out of it. I hadn't worried though. For some reason, Mom tolerated Freddie telling her what to do, when she needed it, where she would have gone ballistic if anyone else had attempted to do the same.

They both had emerged in the kitchen, Mom kind of groggy and Freddie full of life.

'Now you sit down here, my dear,' he had said to Mom, 'and Jo and I are going to rustle up some dinner. I'm inviting myself over; it's the only way a poor overworked civil servant like myself is going to get a break tonight.'

So we had ended up having dinner together, Freddie managing in his way to make us all laugh by the time he had left two hours later. It wasn't perfect, it was never going to be perfect, but it was going to be interesting and maybe that was better.

'Jo, can you pick up where Jason left off?' the teacher asked.

I tried to skim the page to find where we were. I looked over at Chris who had the novel up on his screen. He minimised it and then wrote something quickly.

'Page 103,' his voice said.

A few kids giggled, and the teacher opened his eyes wide in surprise. I smiled at Chris in appreciation and then turned the page in my book to begin reading.

It had taken awhile for Chris to figure out how to use the equipment that John set up for him. At first, it took him much longer to say anything, and he would get tired and stop using it altogether. John kept coming in to school every few days though, tweaking his eye-controlled mouse, and helping him to figure out short cuts. The more John helped him, the more he was determined to practise until it worked. He still made lots of mistakes, and he was still asking for improvements, but every day his 'tech' was giving him more of a voice.

I would remember forever the first full sentences that Chris had spoken to me with his new voice. I had come in to have lunch with him, struggling to pull out a chair so I could sit down and set aside the crutches. Chris had just finished a tutorial session with John.

'He's dying to tell you something, Jo,' Florence had said. 'No one else apparently warrants a word until he speaks to you first.'

'Okay, go ahead, Chris,' I had encouraged, excited to finally hear Chris out loud.

He had taken a minute or so to position the cursor over the speak icon and so I had jumped a bit when the voice started to speak.

'Thank you for my voice, Jo. I hope you will be my friend for a long time because I will have a lot to say to you. My first thing to say is, please, please, no more spontaneous trips. I was never in a river before and I don't want to go again.'

I hadn't known that you could laugh and cry at the same time before that moment. The thing I didn't say that day, but

I will yet, is *Thank you for my voice, Chris.* I'm still finding it, but Chris helps me every day. See, my voice is hidden in the things I don't say – and Chris has known that from the beginning.

I had felt I knew Chris before I ever heard him speak, but now, a couple of months later, I knew there was so much more of him to get to know. He was imagining so much for himself. This English class was only the beginning. He would have to prove himself again and again, but I knew he was stubborn enough to take on that challenge.

The class was over now, and so I got up to put Chris's equipment away, before our slow hobble back to the SE wing.

When I looked up from unplugging his computer, there were three girls standing in a group, a couple of desks away. I had sat in class with them every week since September, but I had never really spoken to any of them. I self-consciously continued to put Chris's computer in its case and slung it over the push bars of his chair.

There was some whispering and one of them stood forward as I went to back Chris out of the tight space his chair was in.

'Excuse me,' she said shyly.

'Yes?' I asked.

'We were just wondering,' she continued, 'if it would be all right to say hi to him. I mean, the computer thing is so cool ...'

I looked at Chris. His smile spoke louder than words.

'Sure,' I invited. 'Meet my friend Chris.'

TURN THE PAGE FOR A NOTE FROM

KIM HOOD

I never set out to write a book dealing with 'issues'; usually when I begin to write it's because imaginary people in my head won't stop talking to me – but I don't really know them when I start to tell their stories. So I didn't know what this story was about when I started to write it. I just knew that Jo was unhappy and that I wanted her to get happy. Chris came along after and, to be honest, he was a bit of a surprise.

Though Jo and Chris, and the story they told me, were what compelled me to write the book, there are some definite themes in *Finding a Voice*. You might be interested to find out how I know about some of these themes and why I think they are important. I'll try to answer.

ON NOT FITTING IN

Even though I didn't have any of the challenges Jo faced in her home, I was a kid who never fit – at least that's how I felt. Like Jo, I spent a lot of lunch hours alone, wishing with all of my might that I could figure out how to be 'normal'. I was shy and awkward and odd. Guess what? I'm still odd. I still don't like small talk all that much. I can be an introvert at times. But I'm okay with that. I don't even want to be normal any more. And the truth is, I'm not sure there *is* a normal. Certainly my closest friends are not normal – but I would say we are all interesting!

If you feel at all like Jo does (and I did), please believe me when I say: IT WILL GET BETTER. Really, it will.

I'm not sure exactly how, or exactly when, but hang in there.

And if you aren't like Jo, and you're surrounded by friends and happy as a lark every day at school, will you look out for the Jos and Kims of the world, please? You might find that you like them if you give them a chance.

ON DISABILITY

Though Chris is fictional, his story was inspired by a real-life event.

When I was nineteen I took a summer job working as a group leader at a camp for kids with disabilities. One of my first groups of campers included a boy who had no use of his arms or legs and couldn't talk. Not much information was given to us about him. I assumed he couldn't understand much.

Each morning there was a breakfast buffet, with lots of choices, but every morning I chose pancakes for this boy, because I thought they would be easiest to swallow and who doesn't like pancakes? Every morning he kept kicking me – until I figured out that he didn't like pancakes. I've now worked with children and adults with various challenges for twenty-five years – and I've tried never to forget that lesson. DON'T ASSUME. It turns out the boy ran a shop in the hospital where he lived. He was better at math than I'll ever be. He usually used a communication device, but he didn't have it with him at camp as it was being repaired.

Everyone has a story that you can't possibly appreciate and understand unless you take the time to know them. DON'T ASSUME. Get to know someone different from you. You might find you have more in common than you think.

ON MENTAL ILLNESS

Like Jo's mum, most of the people with mental illness I have supported have been interesting, complicated people. Mental illness is an area that has always fascinated me, probably because people's experiences are more often different than they are the same. For some people, like Jo's mum, there is something amiss that medication may help alleviate, but IT'S COMPLICATED. In one way or another life is COMPLICATED for everyone isn't it? The most important thing is to accept people for who they are.

ON NON-TRADITIONAL FAMILIES

I guess you could say I grew up in a traditional family. I had a mum and a dad and two sisters (still do). We all lived together. Normal right?

Now my family includes my partner, my daughter and my stepdaughter who lives on another continent with her mum. I know kids with one parent, no parents, two parents of the same gender. Normal right?

As a grownup (well as grown up as I'm going to get, which isn't that grown up) I seem to have a lot of conversations about family. As different as families are, everyone experiences good and bad within their own. Whatever your experience, there is someone out there who relates. THERE IS NO NORMAL, but underneath it all we all care about a lot of the same things.

***

These themes are ones that have woven their way through my life and so it isn't surprising that they emerged in *Finding a Voice*. As the saying goes, 'write what you know' and I guess I did just that.

You can find me at kimhood.com.